HIDDEN LIES

VICTOR WATSON

CATNIP BOOKS
Published by Catnip Publishing Ltd
14 Greville Street
London EC1N 8SB

This edition first published 2012
1 3 5 7 9 10 8 6 4 2

A CIP catalogue record for this book is available from the British
Library.

ISBN 978-1-84647-146-9

Printed in Poland

www.catnippublishing.co.uk

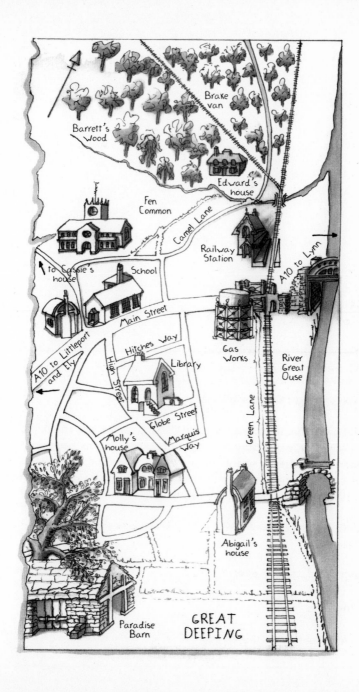

In the summer garden there is an open-air theatre – a large grassy space walled in by high hedges. There are chairs arranged in rows and most of them are occupied. Latecomers are making their way slowly towards their places, carrying cushions and rugs.

At the far end there is a raised grassy stage. Behind it, thick trees and shrubs hide the backstage area from the inquisitive eyes of the audience.

The scene is fixed in time. No one who sees it will ever forget.

The tops of the surrounding trees are touched by the evening sun and a song thrush is improvising from the tip-top of a poplar. A solitary American Flying Fortress crosses the sky at such a high altitude that it seems to be without sound.

Members of the audience – many in uniform – talk among themselves, wave to friends, and unwrap rugs and shawls. But those facing the empty stage are arrested by the sudden appearance there of an unexpected character.

She seems at first to be a young woman. But, no, she is a girl of twelve or thirteen. She is wearing a green shirt and lemon-coloured shorts, and she has long bare legs. She edges sideways onto the stage, furtively, as if she is skulking, trying to hide. She hasn't seen the audience behind her.

Her hair is unruly and she is wild and disordered. The people in the front rows grow hushed, and stare.

Is this part of the programme?

Has the play started?

Is she a kind of prologue?

A hush spreads quickly to the rest of the auditorium and the whole audience watches expectantly.

At that moment the girl turns and sees them. The shock of discovering that she is being watched by several hundred people affects her strangely. She bends awkwardly at the waist, clenches her fists at her mouth as if to stifle a cry, and makes an ungainly movement backwards.

A few people in the audience clap uncertainly. Others laugh. This is clowning of a high quality.

Then, unexpectedly, the girl runs to the front of the grassy stage, and jumps down into the auditorium. She races along one side of the audience and disappears through an arched doorway in the hedge.

The audience applauds.

But one of them just stares. Young Edward Barrett – at the end of the third row – has seen that the girl's face was as white as a sheet. Who is she? She's frightened, he is sure of that. And he is certain she wasn't acting.

1
Legalised Theft

It was such a lovely May morning that Molly Barnes went into the backyard to clean her teeth in the sunshine and admire the tulips at the same time.

Her mother called from the kitchen door. 'Molly! Adam's overslept. Go and get him out of bed, please, love, or he'll miss his train.'

Molly went indoors, rinsed her mouth at the kitchen sink, and took a glass of water with her. She clomped noisily upstairs, intending to pull Adam's blankets off the bed and pour cold water on his feet if he didn't get up at once. She could be ruthless about such things.

But she found him washed and dressed, and sitting at his table, writing. 'I'm finishing my lines,' he said.

Adam had come home from school the day before with an indignant story to tell. 'Teachers shouldn't be allowed to confiscate things,' he grumbled. 'It's stealing.'

He'd tried to explain this to Mr Lawrence, his maths teacher. 'I know it's against the rules for me to have chewing-gum here,' he'd said. 'But that doesn't give you the right to confiscate it for yourself.'

Mr Lawrence liked Adam and he didn't mind being teased.

'*And*,' Adam went on, 'if *you* take the chewing-gum, *you'll* be breaking the rules too. So you should also be writing a hundred lines.'

'You expect *me* to write a hundred lines for *you*?' Mr Lawrence had said, wanting to be clear.

'There's no point,' said Adam. 'You can hand yours in to me, and I can give them back to you. That way I shan't have to do mine. Or, better still, we let them cancel each other out – and neither of us has to write any.'

Mr Lawrence had laughed and said, 'Well, at least that sounds mathematical.'

But Adam still had to write *I must not bring chewing-gum into school* one hundred times. He wrote *I* a hundred times vertically, then *must* a hundred times beside it, and so on. He was quick at it. *Chewing-gum* took longer. He was putting in the final hundred full stops when Molly came in.

'But I still say,' he muttered, 'they don't have the right to confiscate things. It's legalised *theft*.'

Was he serious? Molly wasn't sure. Confiscation was a fact of life – at the boys' school, at Molly's school, and at every school in the land.

Breakfast took ten minutes – cornflakes, and a fat spoonful of golden syrup slowly dripped and melted into the hot milk. Delicious! And then poached eggs on toast. Even with wartime rationing, there was no shortage of eggs in Great Deeping because almost everyone kept chickens. (*You can't get eggs here*, Adam's dad had said in his latest letter from London. *Not for love nor money.*)

As they were gathering up their things, Abigail Murfitt arrived at the door. She lived further along the street, in the railway house beside the level crossing. They set off together, the girls into town to get their bus to Ely, and Adam towards the railway station to catch a train to Soham.

At the station he would meet his young friend, Edward. 'Edward's going to see a play tonight,' Adam said.

'Where?'

'Somewhere in Ely. He's taking his granny. It's her birthday.'

They went their separate ways. Girls were converging from every street, crowding quietly at the bus stop by the church. The church clock struck eight, and the approaching bus could be heard in the distance.

Abigail peered over the churchyard wall. 'Look,' she said quietly.

There was a freshly dug grave, with a pile of brown earth and some turves. The gravedigger was already there, laying down a piece of green carpet to make everything look tidy.

'Someone's going to be buried,' Molly said.

After Uncle Peter's funeral there was a party. The guests trooped slowly back to the house to eat cucumber sandwiches and fairy cakes in the garden. They stood in sombre groups, their black clothes incongruous in the afternoon sun.

That's what happened after a funeral service. Even in 1944, with food rationing.

The guests were mostly people from the town, and they ought to have been sharing respectful memories of Uncle Peter, but their talk was mostly concerned with the girl, Cassie. *What a way to dress!* they murmured to one another. *Fancy turning up at her uncle's funeral wearing sandshoes, shirt and shorts! Had no one told her she should have worn black?*

And, more interestingly, *Where was she to live now? Who would have her?*

'Where has she been since he died?' one of them asked.

'Here,' someone explained. 'Peter's housekeeper has been looking after her.'

'But what's going to happen to her now?'

Heads were shaken, faces were grave. Miss Jardine was getting on, she could hardly be expected . . .

People huddled closer. Was it true that the vicar had offered her accommodation until her future was settled? And that his wife had refused because she hated the girl?

The hatred was mutual, apparently. Cassie disliked the vicar's wife because she bossed Uncle Peter about. *And* Cassie! She used to be quite fond of the vicar but now she despised him because he allowed his wife to be such a horrible person.

That's what they talked about, these funeral guests – with voices lowered and eyebrows raised. They didn't know that Cassie had talked to Uncle Peter about her contempt for the vicar and her dislike of his wife. She always told him everything. *Everything*. 'Why can't she leave me *alone*?' she'd said.

'You will have to learn,' Uncle Peter had explained, 'that you exist in other people's eyes as an object in their lives. It's impossible to be invisible – as I have sometimes found, to my cost.'

Well, Uncle Peter should know. Hadn't he been a British Agent in Germany before the War? Dangerous work, that. But he'd given up being a spy to come home and look after Cassie when she was a baby. And there he had stayed. (Except once, just before the War started.)

Munching their sandwiches and sipping their drinks, people began to wonder where Cassie had hidden herself. *She should be here*, they said, *among the mourners*. Miss Jardine, busy at the tea urn, just sighed and said sharply that you might as well ask where the moon was.

Cassie hadn't been seen since part way through the funeral service. She had followed the coffin dutifully enough, despite her ridiculous get-up. But then she had suddenly jumped to her feet, moved into the aisle, and stood close to the head of the coffin, glaring at it. The vicar fell silent.

'I can't *stand* this!' she shouted at Uncle Peter's coffin. 'And you wouldn't stand it either, if you weren't so *dead*!'

She'd heard the gasps.

Disgraceful!

What a way to behave!

What did she say?

She turned and ran towards the great west door at the back of the church, desperate to get out.

Her voice went right through me!

Such a scene!

But she did love him, you know. And she has no one else.

She'd raced to the back of the church and out into the sunlight. The big west door crashed heavily shut – and Cassie was gone. Someone should have followed her – but they weren't family, those guests, and they felt it was none of their business. The only true relative was a ninety-year-old uncle who thought he remembered Peter as a little boy but had no idea who Cassie was. Besides, if he'd tried to run after her there would probably have been another funeral.

The Vicar sighed, his wife glared – and the funeral continued to its gloomy conclusion without its chief mourner.

'How did she come to have that ridiculous name?' someone asked.

'It's a Greek name,' Uncle Peter had said. 'Your mother and father were very much in love, and they went to Greece for their honeymoon. You were conceived there. You were made in great love and joy.'

Cassie was six at the time of this conversation.

Uncle Peter was direct and truthful. He'd tried hard to be both father *and* mother to her. So over the years he told her everything he knew about girls and women. And conceiving babies.

Cassie trusted him – absolutely.

3
The Man in Cassie's Bedroom

Cassie stopped for a moment in the churchyard, warmed and dazzled by the afternoon sun, breathing hard, and aware of her racing heartbeat. She heard, coming faintly from inside the church, the voice of the vicar resuming his prayer. With the underside of her wrists she dashed away the tears from her face and set off at a run.

Among the tombstones she raced, breathless and fast. *I'm not running properly*, she thought angrily. Ever since they'd told her about Uncle Peter she had been clumsy. Awkwardly, almost falling, she vaulted the low wall and tore across the cricket pitch towards Uncle Peter's house. The backyard gate was open. She went through it like a shot, and hardly slowed as she raced up the path to the back door.

That too was open. As it should be. As it always was in summer.

She was seized by a longing for the safety of her bedroom and the darkness under her bedclothes. Nevertheless, in the kitchen she stopped and stood motionless and quiet for a moment. If only the house would be *different*! But it was exactly the same – and that made it worse that Uncle Peter wasn't there any more.

Quietly she went upstairs and turned towards her room. *Into* her room . . .

Standing near the foot of her bed was a man, a stranger.

For a few crazy fractions of a second they stared at one another. Cassie took in the fact that he had thick black eyebrows and that he was looking through the contents of her chest of drawers, the second drawer down, where she kept her petticoats and underclothes. 'Who are you?' she screamed at him. 'What are you doing in my room?'

He made as if to approach her, but she turned and fled. On the landing she saw that the big bookcase against the wall had been pulled forward, and from the end of it – from behind it perhaps – a woman appeared. She was big – not fat, but *big*, and strong. She stepped out to prevent Cassie from passing, but Cassie shouldered into her and hurtled past, and down the stairs.

Even then it was not over. There was another man in the kitchen, coming hurriedly out as she raced past. She saw that the front door was shut and she would be trapped if she went that way. So she grabbed a doorpost and swung herself round on it before stumbling towards the back door, which was still open.

Round the side of the house she raced, to where she'd left her bike against the front garden wall. She hadn't touched it since the day they'd told her, when

Miss Jardine had said 'Cassie, I'm afraid I have some bad news . . .'

That memory flickered weirdly in her mind as she grabbed the bike, stepped astride it, and pushed off. The bike, which had always seemed like a natural extension of her body, did not respond with its usual grace. It felt heavier than usual. *Nothing* felt the same!

She gathered speed, clumsy and uncertain. But when she looked back there was no sign of pursuit.

Yet.

But where should she go?

She had no friends in Great Deeping. That was the price she paid for going to a school several miles away. She knew she could lie low until the funeral was over and then seek the help of the vicar and his hateful wife. But she would rather die first!

Is there something to do with funerals that nobody told me about? she wondered. *Does this always happen, strangers entering the house of the dead person while everyone else is in church? Was she making a fuss about nothing?*

These were not thoughts. They didn't stay in her head long enough to be worked out. They were like shouts inside her head, silently yelling at her.

She headed for the road to Ely – because that was where she went to school and it was the only road she knew that led out of town. This was not exactly a choice; just desperation coming into focus.

The cycling calmed her. It was the first time she'd been out of the house for a week, since the day Uncle Peter had died. All that time, she'd stayed indoors, either in bed or sitting in the front room doing jigsaw puzzles. Endless jigsaws.

She looked behind her, afraid of pursuit. But there was nothing on the empty road except the local bus from Deeping to Ely. As it overtook her, Cassie saw the passengers staring out at her, disapproving.

Look at that girl! What a sight!

Did you see those shorts?

Shouldn't she be at her uncle's funeral?

Those legs! She don't know what to do with them!

She should cover them up, that's what she should do! They're indecent!

She knew they probably hadn't said any such thing. But she felt super-sensitive, a hundred times more aware than usual of being looked at. She didn't want to be seen at all, not by anybody. But Uncle Peter's words came into her head. *None of us is invisible, as I have found to my cost.*

Two army motorcyclists overtook her, riding side by side, outriders for a military convoy. They were erect on their machines, trim and full of purpose. Then came the trucks, each towing a massive field gun and carrying twenty or thirty soldiers in the back, who whooped and whistled at Cassie, grinning. One raised his rifle and made as if to shoot her.

There had been convoys and troop movements all

through the winter and spring. Everyone knew that the invasion of France must happen soon. It *had* to, people thought – the War had been going on long enough, almost five years. There *must* be a turning point soon. *The Second Front*, they called it. And surely it would happen this summer, as the days grew longer.

But at that moment Cassie cared nothing for the War, or the invasion of France. But how she wished she hadn't put on those lemon shorts! The men whooped and laughed and wolf-whistled. Then she had a brainwave.

She jumped off her bike and stood to attention at the side of the road, saluting. Truck after truck went slowly past her. There was no more wolf-whistling. The soldiers cheered and waved when they saw her, and some saluted back.

The last truck in the convoy stopped. 'Want a lift, love?'

Why not, Cassie thought. 'I'm going to Ely!' she shouted back.

She passed up her bike to the men at the back of the truck, and eager hands reached down to pull her up.

'This is against army regulations,' one of them told her. 'To hell with regulations!' another said.

Cassie wondered if these men knew where they were going. She was tempted to ask, but thought better of it. You weren't supposed to talk about that sort of thing.

But they cheered her up, those soldiers. She told them she'd lived with her uncle and that he'd died.

And that she didn't know what was going to happen to her. '*We* don't know what's going to happen to *us*!' one of them said – and they'd all laughed. They knew they were going into battle; some of them would be killed, almost certainly. And yet they laughed.

She didn't notice another bus, a red double-decker, coming the other way, from Ely. Normally she would have been on that bus herself, coming home from school surrounded by about thirty girls from the High School, silent and apart because of her different school uniform.

That afternoon Molly and Abigail walked out of their school in Ely, carrying their satchels stuffed with homework – and wishing it was the next day instead.

There was one more school day to go before the Whitsun half-term holiday.

For now though, they did what they did every day. The school bus was already waiting at the roadside, and girls were pushing their way onto it. The driver was Molly's Auntie Phyllis and she gave them a friendly wave. Molly joined the crowd, forced her way on board, found a seat, and saved one next to her.

Abigail meanwhile hurried into the newsagent's next to the school and bought a copy of the *Daily Mirror*.

The bus coughed itself into life and Abigail – just in time – jumped aboard and pushed her way to the seat that Molly had saved. Molly took the newspaper and folded it away carefully in her satchel.

They completed their French homework almost as neatly as usual despite the swaying and bumping of the bus, each making one deliberate (and *different*) mistake in case they were accused of copying. You had to be cleverer, they thought, to make a good deliberate mistake than to get everything right.

Working with their books resting on their satchels, they were too preoccupied to notice a girl wearing lemon-coloured shorts climbing into the back of an army lorry. They did see the convoy but paid it no attention. Army convoys had been ten-a-penny that spring. And besides, they were thinking about something else.

They were halfway up their school, these two, but they were as eager and excited as ten year olds that afternoon. They'd been given permission by their mums – against their expectations – to spend a few nights in Paradise Barn. They'd been looking forward to it for days. The girls were to share the single bed, and Adam would sleep on a mattress on the floor.

'My mum has bet your mum that we'll only last one night,' Abigail said.

'Mine thinks we might manage two,' Molly replied.

'Well, we'll prove them both wrong. We'll stay all four nights!'

Molly inwardly hugged herself with anticipation. All four nights of the Whitsun holiday!

There was still one more school day to be endured, but first – tonight! – there were preparations to be made. A mattress had to be carried from Molly's mum's guest house across the fields to the barn. Blankets and pillows too. A bucket of coal, and some kindling. And, of course, as much food as they could get hold of.

They had spent hours in their private room in the barn. They had been there (against the rules) at night.

23

And Adam had slept there on his own. But they had never all three of them slept there. It was a promise of bliss, a sweet plump pleasure to look forward to, like a ripe cherry held in the mouth, still to be bitten into.

But everything had almost gone wrong. For Molly had disgraced herself. Some kind of punishment would inevitably follow, she'd thought.

Molly's mum ran the only guest house in Great Deeping. There were very few guests because of the War. But a few days ago a new visitor had arrived to stay. Molly had been there, standing shyly in the shadows while Mrs Barnes wrote his details in her visitors' book.

'Tittipat, ma'am. Commander Tittipat. T-i-double-t-i-p-a-t, Tittipat.'

'Unusual name,' Mrs Barnes murmured, head bowed over her writing, knowing that if she caught Molly's eye they would both start giggling.

'French, ma'am. My father was of French extraction.' Mr Tittipat was studying his fingertips as if they gave him great pleasure.

'Ah.' Mrs Barnes completed her entry, turned the book around, and asked him to sign in.

Commander Tittipat slowly unscrewed the top of his Swan fountain pen and inspected the gold nib for an unhurried moment or two. Then he wrote his name with an illegible flourish.

'Are you here for business or pleasure?' Mrs Barnes asked. There was no reason why she should have asked him that. There was no wartime regulation requiring her to put that question to him. Nor was she being nosy; she was not a nosy person.

Commander Tittipat carefully replaced the top of his fountain pen and considered his reply. 'Do I look,' he said slowly, 'like the kind of person who could possibly find *pleasure* in a place like this?'

These words were uttered with such icy and venomous malice that Mrs Barnes felt her heart go cold inside her. She no longer felt an urge to laugh.

She would have liked to look him in the eyes, but he wore round spectacles and the thick lenses concealed them. 'How long will you be staying?' she asked.

'A week, probably. Possibly two. I hope no longer than that. Can you direct me to the house of Mr Cheadle?'

'No,' Mrs Barnes said.

Molly was deeply shocked. Of course her mother knew where Mr Cheadle's office was! And of course Mr Tittipat knew that she knew. He sighed, and asked to be shown to his room.

That wasn't the end of it.

Molly – acting as a waitress – had found herself taking him his first breakfast, starting with a tray with teapot, hot-water jug, and cup and saucer. She'd lowered it carefully onto his table and stood back, pausing a moment. She was waiting for the expected thank you. She didn't know she was doing that; it was an unconscious habit. But everyone always said thank you.

But not Mr Tittipat. Not a word, not even a nod of the head. Nothing.

But later, when she took in his sausages and egg and toast, he did speak. 'I expected bacon,' he said, in that creaky voice of his.

Molly blustered a little, stumbling out those words that everyone used at times like this. 'There's a War on,' she said.

'Surely there are pigs in Great Deeping,' he said.

Did he expect a pig to be specially slaughtered so that he could have bacon for breakfast? That was what Molly thought, but what she said was, 'There *are* pigs in Great Deeping. From time to time.'

It was a very rude thing to say. Molly was not usually good at sharp retorts. But she realised – as he stared at her with those cold glassy eyes – that she had implied that Mr Tittipat was a pig.

Which he was, she told herself later. Worse *than a pig, in fact.*

Later, she confessed to her mum what had happened, just in case Mr Tittipat did too. But he said nothing about it. And Molly – who had disgraced herself – was *not* punished by Mrs Barnes, who had been just as rude herself.

Their planned stay in Paradise Barn was safe. But it had been a near thing.

5

Cassie's Favourite Teacher

Cassie was desperate. *I must find Dame Lily*, she thought.

Her full name was Dame Lily Fanshawe-Smith, and she was Cassie's English teacher.

Dame Lily was adored by her pupils. She frequently lost piles of unmarked prep, or added up their examination marks wrongly; and if she went to find a book from the English stock cupboard you could be sure that forty copies of *Oliver Twist* would fall on top of her. Everybody laughed at her, and she laughed at herself.

But if you were being bullied, or if you were a boarder and felt homesick, or if you had a private embarrassment that you couldn't share with the other girls, you knew you could confide in Dame Lily.

The St Dorothea's Boarding School for Girls was not her only interest. She and her brother lived in a large house on the very edge of Ely – next door to the school – and one of her Victorian great-grandparents had spent thousands of pounds on a massive garden, which Dame Lily kept going, despite the fact that her gardeners had been called up for the War.

It was an extraordinary garden – and in the middle

was a grassy open-air theatre. For Dame Lily's other passion was drama. Twice every summer she directed lavish Shakespearean performances in which the main parts were played by actors from the London stage. The first of these annual productions always took place in the early summer, before the exams, so that the more talented girls from St Dorothea's could also take part.

She persuaded people to come from far and wide to attend these plays. There would be academic types from the Cambridge colleges, air-force types from the local RAF hospital (such *nice* officers!), and working-class types (bless them, the poor dears!) from the miners' convalescent home at Littleport. People came in their hundreds, and – since Dame Lily was friendly with the Mitford sisters and lots of well known artists – some of these people were very famous.

Dame Lily was a close friend of Uncle Peter's. In fact, more than a close friend. Once, after Dame Lily had been to tea, he had confessed to Cassie that he'd asked her to marry him several times. Once a year in fact. Cassie, who'd been seven at the time and very possessive, fervently hoped that Dame Lily would go on refusing so that she could keep Uncle Peter to herself.

'Wouldn't you like me to get married?' he'd asked her.

'No, I would not!' she declared. 'Abso-bloomin-lutely *not*!'

Cassie liked Dame Lily, but not quite as much as everyone else seemed to. *I'm a bad jealous person*, she

28

told herself. But why hadn't Dame Lily been at the funeral?

She rang the rusty iron bell beside the porticoed and massive front door. When Dame Lily's brother, Sir Tristram, opened it, wiping soup from his Earl Kitchener moustache, all he could say was what he said to every caller at that time of year, 'I expect she's at the theatre, you know. Go and find her, my dear. Try not to get lost!'

Lavender brushed her bare legs, bumblebees boomed heavily in the rich evening light, and long arching rose stems pinged on the spokes of her bicycle wheels. There were people moving unhurriedly along the broad path that led to the theatre, like a distant crowd in an old painting. Not wanting to be seen because she knew she looked a mess, she stood her bike against a sundial and crouched behind a trellis.

She knew the way to the theatre because on fine summer days Dame Lily took her English classes across from the school and into the garden to read poetry.

There was Prater, the school groundsman, crossing the end of a garden avenue. She disliked him, all the girls did, partly because he insisted on being called *Sergeant* Prater even though he was no longer in the army; but mostly because he was so full of anger. No one knew why.

Sergeant Prater had an orange-brown beard, neatly trimmed and bristly. It didn't grow downwards like normal beards but was thrust forward from his chin like a small pointed shovel. It was so rigid, this beard, that you could imagine him turning sausages in a pan with it, or using it as a fish slice. And he always held his back straight and his head unnaturally high, emphasising the thrustiness of his beard.

The sergeant stood still to light his pipe, filling it with tobacco, patting it firmly down, and greedily sucking the match flame into the bowl.

Cassie ducked out of sight and crept around the outer edge of the theatre, keeping close to the massive yew hedge. She became aware of a murmur of voices coming from the other side of it – a growing audience talking contentedly to itself.

Dame Lily would be backstage, with the actors. She always did that – she would stay backstage until the play had got going and then she would slip away and join the audience at the back.

A man was walking towards her along a wide grassy path between two unruly flower borders. A strange-looking man, she thought. He walked slowly, and after a few steps he paused, leaned stiffly forward and inspected his left toecap. After a few more steps he repeated the action, this time studying his other toecap. He wore a light suit and a homburg hat, and when he raised his head he looked directly at Cassie. She thought for one ghastly moment that he had no eyes. Then she saw that he wore glasses with thick round lenses.

On seeing her he raised his left arm as if to beckon

someone forward. Almost at once a figure appeared beside him, his black hair and thick dark eyebrows unmistakable. It was the man who'd been in Cassie's bedroom.

There was no escape, no empty path where she could make a dash for it. Cassie had never felt so exposed, so ill-dressed and dishevelled, so painfully *there* as an observed and visible object, bright and radiant against the dark hedge behind her.

In a panic she crashed through the shrubs, pushing her way beside the high hedge. Her progress was so difficult that she had no time to see if the men were following her. Then, miraculously, she came to a hole in the hedge – not a doorway, just an unofficial gap – and in an instant she was through.

There were people everywhere – people in costume, people with wigs, people having their make-up put on, and people staring intently into mirrors. Many had roughly bound scripts in their hands and were hurriedly going through their lines.

Two girls from St Dorothea's were huddling, shoulder to shoulder. 'It's all very well for you!' Cassie heard one of them say. 'It's worse for me.'

'Why is it worse for you? We all have our lines to speak.'

'Yes, but you have only two. I have *three*!'

Cassie stumbled among them, feeling self-conscious

and grubby. Then she saw Dame Lily, wearing an ankle-length, dusky-red gown and moving slowly and happily among her troupe, spreading calm and reassurance to everyone she spoke to. She saw Cassie, frowned briefly as if she'd remembered something, and gave her a vaguely troubled wave.

Then Cassie knew it was hopeless. There wasn't the slightest chance of a private talk with Dame Lily.

A young man with a mandolin followed her about, all the time singing in a high, strange voice.

'Tell me where is fancy bred,
Or in the heart or in the head?'

The world had gone mad! Cassie felt as if she were being mocked and tormented, driven crazy by this persistent singer with his whining voice and his foolish tilted head. Then out of the corner of her eye she saw the man with the spectacles making his way calmly through the backstage confusion. His companion followed him, the man with the thick eyebrows.

She fled. Round the edge of the shrubbery, backing her way, stage right, taking the only escape route.

Then she turned – and saw that she was on stage. And there were several hundred people watching her with puzzled interest.

It was the last straw. She ran to the edge of the grassy platform, leapt down into the auditorium and made for the nearest exit in the yew hedge. As she ran she took in the fact that there was an empty seat at the end of the third row, with a boy sitting next to it. He stared at her as she raced past. Why was he staring at her like that? She was *tired* of being stared at!

She plunged desperately through the arched doorway and disappeared into the leafy depths of Dame Lily's garden.

∽

Edward Barrett saw three players walk on stage, one leading the way. Around him, the audience quietened and people settled themselves into their seats.

'In sooth, I know not why I am so sad:
It wearies me . . .'

The voice of the actor was clear and thin in the huge summer evening.

The second character spoke.

'Your mind is tossing on the ocean . . .'

Edward's mind was not tossing anywhere. It was focused on that amazing girl with the long radiant legs who had just raced past him and disappeared into the garden. He strained his ears in an attempt to hear whether she was still out there.

Then he heard a yelp. A short, half-suppressed cry of fear.

He hesitated no longer. He left his seat, and in an instant he was through the arch and out of the theatre. Here, there was a silent enchantment, a soft green-shadowed stillness. The play and its audience seemed to have vanished into a distant universe.

He saw at once the luminous flash of her lemon-yellow shorts in the shadows where she crouched. She was staring at him, wide-eyed.

In an instinctive movement, he put his finger to his lips. It meant, as it always does, *don't make a sound!* But it also signalled: *I'll help you. Trust me.*

It was a fairy-tale moment, touched with magic. But it was also touched with danger, which might or might not be real. Edward didn't know.

There was a plump gentleman ambling along the path that led from backstage. He strolled as if he were enjoying an evening walk in Paris, or Florence. With him was a dark-browed wiry man who darted his eyes from side to side and peered angrily into the undergrowth.

Edward saw the girl crouch lower, making herself small. One hand was clenched to her mouth. She was certain to be seen as the men rounded the bend.

Beyond the path where the two men were walking there was a wooden summerhouse with a small glass window. Now Edward was useless at most sports; he hated football and cricket, and at school he was rarely asked to play in a team. But at home he spent hours throwing a tennis ball against the wall of his house, and catching it. Throw and catch, throw and catch, hour after hour. Now, he was a skilled catcher and an accurate thrower.

Among the leaf litter at his feet was a flint stone, smaller than a tennis ball but exactly the right weight. He stooped, straightened, concentrated for a moment on his target, and threw the stone high, wide and elegant.

At the sound of exploding glass the two men froze and the voices of the actors rose clear and faint from the other side of the hedge.

The dark-browed man hurried off in the direction of the summerhouse. The other stood still and looked calmly around him before slowly following his companion.

Edward hurried to the girl, took her hand and helped her from her hiding place.

'Where's your bike?' he said quietly.

'How do you know I have a bike?' she said, instantly suspicious.

'I was on the bus that overtook you.'

'Oh.'

'Do you need help?' His eyes were level with her mouth.

'I can't go home!' she said. 'I've nowhere to go!'

He ought to have asked her why she couldn't go home. But Edward was under a spell. The world he knew was no longer what it had been; it had this girl in it, who needed his help.

'I have somewhere you can go,' he said.

6
Flashback

During the previous winter, Edward had become the owner of a railway. Strange things *do* happen – and this was one of them. Strictly speaking, it was his grandmother who owned it, old Mrs Barrett, but Edward knew that one day it would be his.

The house where he lived with his grandmother was close to the edge of a wood. It was called Barrett's Wood because that too belonged to her. A single railway track ran through it.

It had been abandoned and disused for thirty years. Early in the War an explosion had crippled the line and left a deep crater. That's another story. But the railway company no longer saw why they should pay rent for a line that was cut off from the main railway. So a railway official came down to visit. They would stop paying rent at the end of the year, he explained. 'After that it's yours.'

'But the track?' Edward said. 'Will you take it away?'

'There's a War on,' the official said. 'We haven't the manpower to lift a mile of railway track. You can do what you like with it – it's yours.'

I am probably the only boy in the country – the whole

world even! – to be given a railway line at Christmas, Edward thought. He was in a state of rapture.

On a bitter colourless January morning, Edward – well wrapped up, and carrying two thermos flasks and a parcel of sandwiches – set off into the trees bent on exploration. Adam Swales went with him.

The trees spread as far as the eye could see that morning, grey and leafless. Underfoot the ground was frozen hard. Leaf litter and ground ivy had slowly gathered over the wooden sleepers until everything was covered except the surface of the metal tracks. The old railway line was being slowly buried.

In the deepest part of the wood, half hidden in the silent trees, they found an old brake van abandoned on the line. It was the kind that freight trains always had at the rear end, where you might see the train guard standing on the platform at the back, watching the passing countryside.

'Cripes!' said Adam. *Abigail would like to see this*, he thought. Abigail, whose mum worked for the railway, was interested in anything to do with trains.

They approached it slowly, hardly believing their eyes. The guard's van was stained with moss and lichen, but it stood there trimly, solid and inviting, and Edward's heart went out to it. All those years it had stood there, waiting for him.

The two boys stood motionless, gazing at the brake van. Adam put his hand on the younger boy's shoulder, allowing him his moment of delight.

At each end there was an open-air platform, like a small travelling balcony. Behind the platform there was a sliding door, with windows. And – best of all! – a small round chimney protruded from the roof, promising snugness.

In less than a couple of minutes they were inside, breathing a smell of long-damp wood. Here there was more to delight them – a small table fixed to the floor, and an upright armchair. And someone had built a wooden bedplace where you could put a mattress. In one corner there was a small iron stove, rusty but otherwise perfect. An oil lamp hung on a hook from the roof, a bucket and shovel stood by the stove, and there was a pile of old newspapers (dated 1936) on the table.

Outside, a few yards further down the line, stood a single abandoned freight wagon. They clambered up the sides to peer in and found to their great joy that it was more than half full of coal. It was damp and mossy, with tufts of grass growing on it. But they knew at one glance that there was enough coal there to keep that stove burning into that far-away future that few children bother about.

'Does *that* belong to you as well?'

'I suppose so,' Edward said cautiously. 'The railway company doesn't seem to want it.'

In such a place they might almost have found a beautiful princess turning straw into gold. But the stove, with all its promise, was almost as good. Better, in fact. 'Do you think we could get it burning?' Edward said longingly.

He was like that, Edward. He never believed that any of his ideas would amount to anything.

Adam – older and protective of the younger boy – said, 'Let's try.'

The kindling they gathered under the trees was damp; the coal was damp; and the newspapers were damp. So it took the boys four attempts to get a fire going in the stove. When they finally succeeded, Edward went outside to watch the smoke pouring out of the chimney, thick, white and satisfying. His guard's van had come to life.

Once lit, the stove whispered softly to itself. Almost immediately it became too hot to touch, the windows steamed up, and the inside of the van grew slowly warm.

'It needs a few finishing touches,' Edward said cautiously. He was pretending to be casual, but secretly he had fallen in love. His life story was full of things he had fallen in love with – a book, a model train, a tiny toy Spitfire.

Outside, it started to snow. Inside, a small church window in the side of the stove glowed red. The two boys ate their sandwiches, Adam seated at the table, Edward on the bedplace. Enchantment settled around them, among the grey trees outside and on the roof above their heads.

But afterwards, while Adam was sketching the stove,

he spotted something under the bedplace. 'What's that?' he said. 'Under where you're sitting.'

There was a leather belt or strap, and Edward pulled out a black bag, a bit like a school satchel.

Eagerly they emptied the contents on the table – a small notebook with nothing written in it; a packet of dark-brown cigarettes; and a fat leather purse. When Adam clicked it open, a flood of silver coins spilled out onto the table.

This was a different kind of magic. When Edward picked one up and studied it, he saw on one side an eagle with outstretched wings holding in its claws a wreath. And inside the wreath there was a swastika.

He dropped it as if its touch might be poisonous, looking anxiously up at Adam. 'It's only a coin,' Adam said.

At the cinema they had seen the Nazi flag hundreds of times – flying above town halls, on great poles flanking Adolf Hitler as he shouted at crowds of adoring supporters, carried in triumph by marching German troops as they paraded through the cities of conquered Europe. The swastika was the fear that lay behind all fears.

But – as Adam said – a coin can hurt no one, and they began to inspect their find more carefully. They found that the coins were identical, each worth five reichsmarks, and they were all dated between 1936 and 1939. They were roughly the size of a British half crown.

They stacked them in piles of ten. *Three* piles of ten.

'Thirty pieces of silver,' Adam said quietly. 'Someone has been betrayed.'

That is why Edward – faced with a girl who was too scared to go home – was able to say those magical words: 'I have somewhere you can go.'

There is no easy way to carry a mattress.

They found it was impossible to get a grip on it. Adam tried balancing it on his head like a wooden board – but it sagged in the middle and enveloped him front and back. And yet, when they tried to fold it and carry it like a big parcel, it wouldn't allow itself to be treated like that.

Two fields away – in the low light of the evening – a solitary walker stopped, watched them for a moment or two, and slowly raised his hand in distant greeting. It was farmer Morton, who owned the barn. 'He might have come over and helped!' Abigail muttered.

But eventually they completed the journey across the fields and dragged the rebellious mattress over the floor of the shadowy barn and up the stairs. Abigail brushed earth off the mattress where she'd dropped her end of it, and said firmly, 'Now! What does Daisy do next?'

Every day, they bought the *Daily Mirror* – not for its news but for its strip cartoons. There was a whole page of them. But the one they liked best was about the adventures of the beautiful and accident-prone *Jane*, who always outsmarted the enemy, repeatedly found herself in embarrassing situations, and could be relied on to lose some of her clothes. And quite frequently all of them.

'*We* could write a strip every bit as good as that,' Abigail had said.

That was how the idea had been born – because of *Jane*. 'You could make up the stories,' she'd said to Molly. 'I would do the words. And Adam would draw the pictures.'

Adam had been drawing strip cartoons ever since he could remember. As long as he had a clear story, he could reduce it to six or eight small square frames in half an hour of perfect miniature drawing.

So they'd put their heads together. They needed a name for their heroine.

They thought of Fearless Freda first. Then Harriet the Heroine. Then Gutsy Gertie. Daring Daisy was the next idea, reversed eventually so that Daring became her surname, Daisy Daring. Finally – at Molly's suggestion – she became *Daisy Daring of the Secret Service*. It was settled!

Adam did not draw caricatures. None of his characters had exaggerated chins, or distorted noses, or heads as big as their bodies. Daisy was tall, beautiful and shapely, drawn as if she were real. Molly was secretly impressed that he could draw an entire young woman, perfect, in a small space the size of six postage stamps. What's more, he could draw her in all kinds of outfits, from military uniforms to a barmaid's apron.

Or, like Jane in the *Daily Mirror*, with nothing on at all, stepping into a bath, or taking a midnight dip in a river.

They knew that nakedness was private, not something to be shown to strangers. For that very reason it added a touch of mischief to Daisy Daring's adventures.

In twenty-two episodes Daisy had:

~ parachuted into France and landed in a heap of pig-manure;

~ rescued a British prisoner of war only two minutes before he was to be shot by a firing squad;

~ destroyed an entire enemy convoy by disguising herself as a German officer and directing the leading truck over a handy cliff top;

~ used her torch to guide British bombers on a night-time raid on an enemy airfield (without getting bombed herself);

~ somehow got herself a lift into Berlin on the back of a motorcyclist taking secret messages to Gestapo headquarters;

~ and infiltrated herself into Berlin society as a Prussian countess.

Now she was to be presented to Adolf Hitler himself at a party in the depths of his secret bunker.

And the reason for Daisy's adventures? It was because British Intelligence knew there was a vital book of secret codes – and that the Führer always carried it in the pocket of his tunic. Daisy's task was to get hold of it, escape from the bunker, and somehow get safely across enemy-occupied Europe and bring the book home.

It wasn't asking much, not for a clever girl like Daisy.

They'd found in Mrs Burnside's stationery shop a blank hard-covered book with unlined pages, perfect for a long-running picture story. It had become worn and shabby because it was regularly passed round at both their schools. Sometimes they lost sight of it completely for a day or two, but it always turned up, restored to them so that the next instalment could be added.

'What happens next?' Abigail said.

'One in the eye for Adolf,' Molly answered at once. She'd been planning it all through school.

So! Four frames:

~ In the first, the lovely Daisy approaching a closed door, with a Nazi guard at each side. She is nervous, you can tell.

~ In the second, the back of the Führer's head in the foreground. At the other end of the room, Daisy walking in. A windowless banquet room, a huge table spread with food and drink. High-ranking Nazis everywhere, all armed.

~ In the third, Hitler and Daisy close, facing each other, seen in profile. A nearby officer whispers into Daisy's ear *Salute him, you Dummkopf!*

~ In the fourth, Daisy cries *Heil Hitler!* and shoots out her right arm in the Hitler salute with such enthusiasm that she pokes the Führer in the eye. His mouth is downturned in a furious scowl, his moustache has jumped clear of his upper lip, and strings of tiny exclamation marks and lopsided swastikas show how angry he is.

~ Caption: ONE IN THE EYE FOR ADOLF.

As Adam drew, Molly could almost see the characters moving before her eyes on the table – tiny, clear, three-dimensional figures, like creatures in a rock pool at the seaside, living, moving and breathing before her eyes. The Nazis were solid and menacing, Daisy bright and brave.

Perfect, she thought happily. There was danger, excitement, and a joke. What more could a reader desire?

The next day Molly and Abigail would take Daisy to school and she would be passed among their classmates.

Two Troubled Men

If Cassie had stayed until after the funeral service she might have noticed that one of the guests was especially unhappy. And not with grief for Uncle Peter.

Mr Marcus Ross was the Great Deeping undertaker. While Cassie was on the bus and Edward was following on his bike, Mr Ross was pacing restlessly around his office.

Who are Caistor & Walkman? he asked himself crossly.

It was his boast that he buried everyone in the town – and would continue to do so until he came to be buried himself. It was unheard of for any family in Deeping to consult an undertaker from somewhere else. Unheard of! Yet Peter Dinsdale's people had done exactly that. Who had ever heard of undertakers called Caistor & Walkman?

He took down from a dusty bookshelf a copy of the national register of undertakers. *Who are Caistor & Walkman when they're at home?* he muttered to himself. However, there they were, properly listed – Caistor & Walkman, Funeral Directors, Kensington.

Kensington? That was absurd! Why choose a firm in London when there was a perfectly good one in your own town? Mind you, they had done a perfectly good job. He had to admit that. Four spotless Rolls Royces (despite petrol rationing), a beautiful oak coffin, and no staggering under the weight.

But the same could not be said, he thought, for the way the death had been handled *before* the funeral. *That* had been very shabby. Everyone knew that a corpse should spend the last few days in its home, lying discreetly in the coffin so that people could call and say how nice it looked.

But Peter Dinsdale's body had *not* been allowed to lie at his home. It had been whisked off by Caistor & Walkman to their funeral parlour in Kensington. *Funeral parlour!* What kind of new-fangled idea was *that*? All a good undertaker needed was an office at the front and a woodworker's workshop at the back. Not a *parlour*.

Ridiculous!

The other troubled funeral guest was Mr Albert Cheadle, a solicitor. Two days after the death of Uncle Peter, he'd received a letter from the housekeeper, Miss Jardine.

Dear Mr Cheadle,

I am writing to you because you are my late employer's lawyer, and because I wish to inform you that I am resigning immediately as housekeeper.

As you know, I took on the job when Mr Dinsdale came back from foreign parts to look after Cassiopoeia when her

48

parents were killed. However, it was never my intention to stay in that job for life and I bought myself a small retirement cottage in Norfolk. Now that the child is left alone again, some new arrangement will have to be made for her care.

Of course I will stay until the day of the funeral and I will arrange refreshments. However, I intend to leave immediately afterwards.

Yours faithfully,
Edith Jardine

'Damn!' Mr Cheadle said softly. 'Damn! Damn! Damn!'

Miss Jardine's letter presented him with a difficulty. He had hoped she would stay on to look after the girl until he could make a more permanent arrangement. Just for a few weeks.

But who would look after her now?

On the bus to Deeping Cassie took herself to task. *I must not give way to self pity*, she told herself. But then she thought: my only close relative is dead; I'm probably going to be put away in an orphanage; I made a fool of myself at the funeral; I found strange people ransacking the house; and two men are hunting for me.

Am I downhearted? Absolutely I am!

On the other hand, she thought, I have a champion, my Hopeless Hero, who looked as if he needed cuddling. ('*How* have you got somewhere I can sleep?' she'd said to him. 'Do you own a *hotel* or something?')

The bus conductor came for her ticket (it was Edward's ticket, but that didn't matter). 'Are you all right, love?' she said.

Cassie grinned at her. 'Abso-bloomin-lutely!'

'That's the spirit,' the conductor said back.

Edward was as good as his word. As the bus drew away and left Cassie in the sudden empty silence at the bus stop back in Deeping, she saw him ghosting like a shadow towards her, riding her bike in the chilly summer twilight.

Shivering and hungry, she cycled behind him to the

other side of town and into a narrow lane. *Where is he taking me?* she wondered. *And why am I so* tired? They came to a solitary house and she saw the thick darkness of a wood ahead of them. The boy dismounted and whispered that they mustn't make any noise.

'Is there somewhere I can sleep?' Cassie felt confused, and weak through lack of food.

'Yes. But not in the house. My gran would find out. She mustn't be worried.'

He wheeled her bike and she followed him round to the back of the house, down a grassy garden, and into the trees at the edge of the wood. Once or twice, where there was a danger of tripping, he switched on a torch and shone it at her feet.

She followed him through the silent trees until a large lump of blackness loomed in front of them. In spite of the darkness she recognised the shape. *One more crazy impossible thing! A railway van in the middle of a wood!*

Uncle Peter's voice came suddenly into her memory, clear as a bell. 'In my experience, there is something unexpected in every forest in the world!' What kind of thing? she'd asked. 'Oh, a house made of gingerbread, or a gibbet with a corpse, or a kindly woodcutter willing to share his bread and cheese.' And she'd known – even then – that that wasn't quite what he meant.

Or a railway van, Cassie thought. Somehow it was comforting. It connected her with Uncle Peter again, briefly.

The boy helped her up to the platform at one end and opened the sliding door. Hugging her shoulders for warmth, she watched him put a match to an oil lamp and slowly, wonderingly, she followed him in, gaping dazedly in the yellowy lamplight – at the table, two chairs, a bed with mattress and a pile of blankets. And some books.

She sat weakly on the bed, watching in a kind of numbness while Edward knelt in front of the stove and set a match to it. It had been laid already, and in a few seconds a small tidy fire was burning.

'Who are you?' she said.

'Edward,' he said. 'I'm Edward Barrett.'

The sight of warmth made her shiver uncontrollably and Edward took a blanket off the pile and said, 'Wrap yourself in this. I won't be long.'

'Where are you going?' She wasn't keen on being left alone.

Wasn't it obvious? 'To get something to eat,' he said.

She frowned in bewilderment.

Edward explained. 'My supper's waiting for me. And there is twice as much as I can eat.'

This was past all comprehension. 'How do you know?'

'Because I got it ready before I went out.' Then, seeing her confusion, he said, 'I live with my gran. Usually, she does all the food and I do everything else. But today she was too tired.'

Cassie crouched as small as she could and tried to

stretch the blanket to cover both her shoulders and her bare legs.

'She was supposed to come to the play tonight. We'd got two tickets for her birthday treat – but she was too tired to go. So I went on my own. She usually goes to bed early now.'

In the rosy silence their words floated slowly free like coloured crystals, carrying their meanings with them.

'Is she ill?'

'Just old.'

Left alone, Cassie knelt on the floor close to the stove and sank into a kind of oblivion, aware only of the loud ticking of a brass clock that stood on a shelf. 'Sometimes,' Uncle Peter had told her, 'when things are really bad, you find that you have unaccountably landed on your feet.' Cassie wasn't sure what she had landed on.

She heard movements outside. Suppose those men had followed her here? But it was Edward. He slid the door open with his foot and came in with a loaded tray. There were thick beef sandwiches, a jar of pickled onions, and a jug of milk.

Cassie stumbled to her feet and pulled up one of the chairs. When the blanket fell to the ground, Edward stooped for it and wrapped it around her shoulders. Then, silently, they ate – and the empty ache in her stomach was slowly appeased. But she shivered repeatedly, uncontrollably.

'Have you run away?' Edward asked her.

'Yup!' She nodded emphatically, crunching a pickle.

'Why?'

It seemed to him that several minutes passed before she answered. 'My uncle died,' she said. 'I ran home in the middle of the funeral – and *the house was full of strangers!*'

'They were looking for something,' she added. 'I was scared!'

'Strangers?'

'Yep! I *can't* go back there!' she said through a mouthful of sandwich.

'I'd better go now,' he said. 'I'll bring you some breakfast in the morning.'

Cassie was glad he was going. She felt vaguely grateful to him – *my half-grown hero*, she thought – but she wanted to be left alone. The day had had too much in it.

'You'd better lie low here all day tomorrow. We shan't be back from school until almost five.'

'*We?*'

'Adam and me. Adam's my friend.'

'But no one else must know where I am!' She spoke imperiously, like a princess giving orders.

But she might as well not have bothered. 'Adam's OK,' he said. 'This is his place as well as mine. He won't tell anyone. He never tells anyone anything!'

Cassie scowled in a way that Uncle Peter would have recognised.

'Besides, if you're really going into hiding, you're

going to need more than just me to help you. For a start, we need to find out who those strange men were.'

That was cheering, Cassie thought, and her scowl vanished. 'Is there a chamber pot?' she asked.

Edward blushed, and Cassie knew at once that these two boys would manage without, just as Uncle Peter would have done.

'But there's some toilet paper,' Edward said proudly. He indicated a wad of newspaper torn neatly into squares and spiked on a meat hook.

At the door he stopped and turned to face her. 'You haven't told me your name.'

She was briefly reluctant. It seemed like giving away something private. *But that's silly*, she told herself. 'Cassiopoeia Covington,' she said. 'Everyone calls me Cassie.'

Edward left, saying over and over to himself *Cassie, Cassie Covington*.

After he'd gone, Cassie put out the lamp and sat on the edge of the bed gazing vacantly at the red glow of the little stove window. The van was warming up and she had stopped shivering. But she was overcome with weariness and doubt. Had she over-reacted? Had she been hysterical and silly? For her new hero had made it clear to her – running away was a serious business.

But what else could she have done? Uncle Peter was the only person who cared about her. And no one had stepped forward and said, 'Come and live with me.'

She remembered something Uncle Peter had told

her. He'd been in a crowded railway station in Berlin. Everything had seemed normal, with people hurrying to and from their trains, others standing by their luggage, or studying timetables. 'Suddenly I was scared,' he said. 'There was nothing I could see to explain it. It was an instinct. So I left the station, crossed the street and went for coffee. And I *watched*. Sure enough, a man came out of the station, followed me across the road and waited outside the café. He had his right hand in his jacket pocket.'

'What happened?' Cassie had asked. Uncle Peter often told her stories.

'Oh, I got away easily enough, through the toilets at the back. But the point is, I hadn't *seen* that man on the station but I *had* been alerted somehow. If you feel an instinctive fear, you should trust it. Your instinct is probably right.'

Uncle Peter kept saying things inside her head. Now – when he was dead and she couldn't ask him – it occurred to her for the first time that he might have made up that story to teach her something. She too had felt instinctively that there was something wrong. You didn't normally expect to find people searching a house while the owner was being buried. *Did* you?

She wished she had some pyjamas. In her grubby shorts and top she lay down on the bed and arranged all four of the blankets on top of her. There was a cushion for a pillow and she found she was suprisingly comfortable.

She expected a troubled night, but she fell asleep immediately and didn't wake for hours.

From time to time Edward allowed himself to pretend that his father was still alive.

He was a good pretender. He would imagine that his grandmother received a telegram saying there had been a mistake: his father, instead of being shot in the War, had been found alive in a Spanish prison. He'd been released and was on his way home.

On one occasion he had acted it out. He'd walked to the railway station in time to meet the evening train from London and bought a penny platform ticket. How, he wondered as he stood on the platform, would a boy and his long-lost father greet each other? Would they shake hands? Or hug? And as they walked home from the station, would they hold hands?

No, he decided. They would just walk side by side, talking quietly, father and son together.

Like all true pretenders, he *never* confused his imagined world with reality. Never! If he was interrupted in his pretending he could switch it off in the blink of an eye.

His favourite pretend narratives were rescue stories. When he had been very little he had imagined himself rescuing small injured animals. Then for a year or two he'd had an invisible friend called Bootsie who lived in an old boot. As he grew older, the stories changed.

He occasionally rescued his grandmother from poverty and set her up in a palace with hundreds of servants.

His grandmother did *not* live in poverty, but he liked to pretend sometimes that she did. So that she could be rescued from it.

He found – as he explored the books in his grandmother's house – that there were lots of stories which ended with a rescue. The best of these were those in which a young prince (or he might be a poor miller's son, it didn't seem to matter) rescued a princess from terrible danger.

So when he found Cassie, distressed and frightened in Dame Lily's garden, Edward knew what he had to do. His real life – for once – had the same shape as his imagined life. He understood that Cassie was no princess. There was another awkwardness too: she was older than he was, and two or three inches taller. It wasn't like that in the stories. But, princess or not, she clearly needed rescuing.

10
A Job for Hilda Pritt

Senior Flying Officer Hilda Pritt piloted the huge Halifax bomber low over Great Deeping, glancing down at the washing lines in people's back gardens to check the wind direction. Then, satisfied, she banked and headed straight for the airfield a few miles away.

She glanced at her wristwatch. 'We might be able to get a late breakfast in the mess,' she said to her navigator. 'I'm starving!'

The plane's huge landing wheels were lowered and the Halifax reduced speed, skimming a cornfield on the boundary of the airfield. Its wheels touched down – gently, gracefully, without the slightest hint of a bounce. Having brought in the big plane with her usual elegance, Hilda taxied towards the hardstanding by the hangar. A few minutes later she was jumping to the ground and greeting young Tom Granger, the mechanic.

'Morning, miss!' Tommy didn't salute her, or call her *Ma'am*. The Air Transport Auxiliary was not part of the RAF and Hilda was, technically, a civilian. Yet she knew that Tommy had as much respect for her as for the other pilots on the station. He'd told her so during an intimate waltz at the Christmas dance in the Constitutional Hall at Great Deeping. And she'd laughed and said, 'Don't be such an *idiot*, Tommy!'

'You have to see the boss, miss,' he said. 'Straightaway. It's urgent, apparently.'

'Oh, I *say*!' Hilda said crossly. 'I've just flown this bally thing practically the entire length of England and I'm jolly hungry!'

'Sorry, miss. That's what I was told to tell you.'

'Well, he can jolly well wait!' Hilda found it hard to concern herself much about Group Captain Rayburn because he'd been a schoolmate of her younger brother. In fact, in the school holidays, when she was about ten she had not infrequently given both boys their bath, put them to bed, and read them stories about Peter Rabbit.

With her parachute held loosely over her shoulder, Hilda set off across the grass. Cocky little devils they were too, she recalled.

Eggs on toast. That was all they could rustle up in the mess at that time in the morning. And a hot coffee. But it was better than nothing and so, having kept the Boss waiting for half an hour, Hilda presented herself at his office.

She found he had a visitor, and the atmosphere was tense.

The stranger was not introduced. He was a civilian, elderly, wearing a dark grey pinstripe suit and waistcoat. Immaculate shining black shoes. She'd seen thousands like him in London. There was the smell of pipe tobacco too. Hilda was not particularly sensitive to emotional

60

atmosphere but she picked up at once that the men were worried and ill at ease with each other.

'Sit down, Hilda. We have something to discuss with you.'

'Gosh! Sounds jolly important.'

Group Captain Rayburn scowled at her. *Don't clown about!*

So Hilda sat primly in front of the two men – with her back straight, her knees together, her hands folded in her lap, and a dutiful expression of attentiveness on her face. She knew exactly what was required of a young woman in the presence of two men in authority.

The man in the suit looked at her with undisguised irritation. He disapproved of women in trousers. Then he began to speak. 'You are familiar with Great Deeping, I believe?'

Hilda nodded. 'I used to stay with my grandmother when I was a child. She lives in the area. And I was on special duties here in 1940.'

'Ever come across a chap called Peter Dinsdale?'

'Never heard of him. Sorry!'

'He used to work for us . . . Secret stuff. Special Ops, that sort of thing. Based in Germany for years before the War. One of our best chaps.'

'A spy,' Hilda said.

The man in the suit ignored that. 'He had to give it up and come home. His sister and her husband were killed in a car crash, and they left a baby girl. Something like that. Anyway, he came home to look after her.'

Admirable behaviour, Hilda thought. *But what's it got to do with me?*

'He died a week ago.'

The man in the suit glanced over to Group Captain Rayburn, handing over to him.

'Hilda, there's a big show coming off soon. You know that. Everyone knows it! Hitler knows it too – but he doesn't know exactly *when* and he doesn't know exactly *where*. But Peter Dinsdale *did* know where and when. I can't tell you why, but take my word for it – he knew every bally thing there is to know about the allied invasion of Europe!'

It took a moment for Hilda to take all that in. 'And he died?'

'Yes, but that's not the point. The point is that his niece has disappeared.'

'What has all this got to do with me?'

The man in the suit replied. 'We want you to look for her,' he said. 'We've arranged for you to be transferred temporarily from ATA duties to work for Special Ops.'

'But I'm due for a week's leave,' Hilda protested.

'You can have your leave afterwards. There's a War on.'

Both men were implacable. And Hilda suddenly lost her cool. 'I fly planes,' she snapped. 'That's my job. I fly Hurricanes, Spitfires, Mustangs, any damn thing I'm asked to fly! This morning I flew a brand-new Halifax down from Lancashire while you were still eating your boiled eggs! That's what I *do*! I *don't* do ruddy missing persons! That's a job for the police!'

But even as she said these things another part of her mind was working out the seriousness of the situation. A girl had disappeared, a girl whose uncle had known the biggest secret of the War – one which Hitler and his generals would give anything to know. By the time she'd reached her last words of protest she realised that she no longer believed what she'd started to say. If they wanted her help, it was her duty to try.

'We have people searching for her, of course,' Rayburn said. 'But you are known in the town. And you're good with children. You sorted out those other little difficulties at the start of the War. Remember?'

Of course Hilda remembered! 'The kids did it all, mostly,' she said. 'I just happened to have a gun when it was needed.'

'Hilda . . .'

'All right! *All right!* I'll do it! Tell me about this bally schoolgirl! How old is she?'

'Thirteen – just.'

'And?'

The man in the suit continued. 'She took off in the middle of the funeral. Went completely to pieces, apparently! Stormed out of the church in the middle of the service and ran back home.'

'When *was* the funeral?'

'Yesterday.'

'Gosh! You haven't wasted much time.'

'We have reason to believe that she found some intruders in the house . . .'

'Intruders?'

'They were looking for something.'

The poor kid must have been terrified, Hilda thought. 'Special Ops?' she asked.

She got no reply to that. 'She managed to get away. Then she cycled out of town.'

'Do we know where she went?'

'She was seen cycling towards Ely.'

'Why Ely?'

'She goes to school there. *Not* the Ely High School. She goes to St Dorothea's Boarding School for Girls, and she has a favourite teacher there who just happens to be a friend of her uncle's. Her name is Dame Fanshawe-Smith. She's been questioned, of course, and she confirmed that the girl did indeed turn up, looking distressed. But she didn't speak to her because she was backstage at a drama thingy she was busy with. The girl disappeared in the crowd, and that's the last anyone saw of her.'

'You want me,' Hilda said slowly, 'to mingle with the children of Great Deeping because kids always know what's going on. Correct?'

She took out a packet of cigarettes and a lighter. The man in the suit probably thought it was an outrageous impertinence; but the man who'd been frequently bathed by her when he was four hadn't the courage to reprimand her.

'I guess the school at Ely is a public school.' Both men frowned. It *was*, but how had Hilda deduced that? 'I doubt,' she said with more than a touch of sarcasm, 'if many ordinary local schools have a dame on their staff.'

'Does it make a difference?'

'It makes it harder. If she goes to a private school ten miles away she'll be more or less unknown to the local kids. They probably won't know anything about her.'

Group Captain Rayburn had had enough of this. He disapproved of negative thinking. 'Well, we want you to try, Hilda. These are difficult times for us all.'

Hilda interrupted him. 'What's the kid's name?'

'Cassiopoeia. Cassie for short.'

When Edward came in that morning, Cassie sat up in bed, staring at him in confusion. He had brought a large plate of toast and a jar of marmalade. 'That's all I could manage,' he said. 'Sorry! But there's plenty of it.' There was a mug of milk too. 'I must go now, or I'll miss my train.'

'Train?' She was bewildered, full of sleep.

'I go to school on the train,' he said.

'Where?'

'Soham,' Edward said. 'I started last September. Adam goes there too. He's higher up the school.'

Soham? Why would boys from Great Deeping go to school in Soham? Surely Soham was miles away? There was so much she didn't know.

Left alone, sitting up in bed, she ate the toast and drank the milk. Then she curled up under the blankets and went back to sleep.

When she awoke the brass clock told her it was almost twelve. She badly needed a pee and there was nothing for it but to get up and go outside. The fire in the stove had gone out during the night, but the wagon was warm in the dappled sunlight. She stepped out into the soft early-summer air and set off into the trees.

How strange it all was.

Later, she turned her attention to Edward's books. One of them was *Robinson Crusoe*, which she'd read without ever being sure whether it was true or made up. Uncle Peter had been no help. 'Everything is fiction,' he'd said.

Typical! she thought affectionately. She took down *Biggles Goes to War* and started to read, willing to believe every word of it.

↾

At around half-past four, she heard voices outside. 'She won't be there, y'know! I bet she's scarpered!'

She heard Edward say, 'She'll be here.' *He's very trusting, she thought. But what about the other one? How would she get on with him?* The next minute the two boys stood one behind the other at the open door. 'Hello,' Edward said, shy because his friend was there.

'I'm Adam,' the newcomer said. He grinned at Cassie and looked at her with unashamed interest. She didn't want him staring at her.

'Supper won't be until six,' Edward said, 'but I've got some biscuits and lemonade for now.'

'His gran does good suppers,' Adam said.

Taller than me, Cassie thought to herself. *A bit.*

The boys gave themselves two biscuits each, Cassie

three. They were in a cheerful frame of mind because it was the start of the Whitsun half-term holiday. They had the weekend, and Monday and Tuesday, to spend how they liked. Four whole days.

They settled themselves, the boys at the table, Cassie on the bed with her knees drawn up. Part of her mind was studying her grubby bare feet. 'How did this wagon thing come to be here?' she asked.

'We found it,' Edward said. 'Nearly a mile further along the track.'

Cassie the princess snapped crossly. 'I meant how did it come to be *here*?' But at once she was ashamed of herself. She saw that Edward didn't know how to deal with bad temper. Uncle Peter had always fought back and they would rage at each other. But this boy just looked hurt.

Why did I speak to him like that?

Patiently Edward explained. 'A friend of ours came home on leave, and his dad's a farmer. We asked him to help us push. But we still couldn't shift it. So he went home and brought back a couple of heavy horses from the farm. Then he harnessed them up and they hauled the van here. There was a coal wagon as well, and the horses pulled that here too.'

'It's nice,' Cassie said quietly. *It really is nice*, she thought to herself.

She found there was a firmness in Edward too. He could be very direct. 'You've got to tell us everything that happened,' he said. 'If you want us to help.'

Help? That sounded promising. So she told them the story. And she found that in the telling, the normal separated itself from the abnormal.

There was nothing strange about a man dying. And it wasn't strange that the shock of it kept hitting her when she least expected it – as she walked past his empty bedroom, or when she saw his toothbrush and shaving things in the bathroom.

It was sad – *very* sad – but not weird.

The intruders, however, were a different matter. 'And in my *bedroom*!' she said indignantly. Her voice squeaked when she said it.

The mystery became more significant when you knew about Uncle Peter's job.

'What *was* his job?' Adam asked.

'He used to be a British agent in Germany,' she said. 'Before the War.' There was no reason why she shouldn't tell them. It was ages ago. 'He gave it up to come home and look after me.'

'Your parents . . .' (*Tricky subject*, Edward thought.)

'They were killed. I was a few months old.'

'And your uncle stopped being an agent then?' Edward asked.

'Yes. He had me to look after. There was no one else in the family.'

'And he didn't go away any more?' (Edward tried to imagine a spy – shabby and unshaven, with mean shifty eyes – cradling a baby in his arms.)

'No. Except once. He said he had to go to Germany.'

'He *told* you where he was going?' (Was it normal for spies to tell people about their missions?)

'Yes.'

'When was this?'

'In 1939. In the summer. He went to Berlin.'

'That was the year the War started,' Adam said, looking up.

Cassie hadn't known Adam was listening. He'd taken out a sketchbook, laid it on the table, and sat – with a pencil in his hand – staring at her legs.

'Adam draws,' Edward explained. 'All the time.'

Was that why he had looked at her so keenly? she wondered. *Because he liked drawing people?*

'Berlin?' Edward said, prompting her.

'He was in Berlin when the War started. He was trapped there.' *Is that boy drawing my legs?* she thought.

'Did he come back?' Edward asked.

'Yup!' she said.

12
Flashback – Christmas Eve, 1939

All over Europe it was a grim Christmas, with thousands of children in danger, or in the wrong homes, or expecting a mean and cut-down festival.

Cassie was only eight then, and she hadn't seen or heard anything of Uncle Peter since July.

She'd woken up shortly before midnight, hearing voices downstairs and doors being opened and shut. For a few confused seconds she thought that Father Christmas had arrived and was chatting to Miss Jardine. Then she'd heard footsteps on the stairs, slow and determined. She raised herself on her elbows and waited, feeling sure that Uncle Peter had come home – at last! At the same time she braced herself for disappointment, unsteadily holding both feelings inside her.

He opened the door and strode across the room. Cassie leapt to her feet and – standing on her bed – threw her arms around him, burying her face in the side of his neck and loving the feel of his arms tightly around her.

'Cass!' he said passionately. With his big hands he'd pushed back her hair so that he could see her face properly.

But it was suddenly too much for her. She stood back and began to hammer his chest fiercely with her fists, angrily and tearfully shouting, 'Where have you *been*? Why have you been away so *long*? It's been *months*!'

As quickly as it had come, her anger evaporated. 'I thought you were dead,' she said.

'So did I.'

Then she saw what she hadn't noticed – his face pale and grey, with a drawn and haggard look. *Oh!* she said inwardly. *He's ill! He's going to die.*

He sat on the edge of her bed then, and she got back under the covers, sitting with her chin resting on her knees, staring at him.

'You know why I had to go. There was something I had to find out – for the government.'

Cassie nodded. She imagined Uncle Peter meeting the king and handing over the secret information in a large brown envelope. And the king saying thank you, slowly because of his stammer.

'It took longer than expected,' Uncle Peter went on. 'I was still there when War was declared. I was trapped.'

'But you escaped.'

'Eventually.' There were some things an eight year old could not be told.

'Was the government pleased?'

Uncle Peter smiled. 'Yes,' he said. 'I think what I told them helped. But Cassie, did you tell anyone where I had gone, or why?'

'No,' she said quietly. 'I promised you I wouldn't. I didn't even tell Tiddly Pom.'

'Good. Some secrets are too important even for teddy bears.'

'Will you have to go away again?'

'Probably not. Certainly not for a very long time.'

She would have to be content with that.

13
Halifaxes and Horsas

'We had a lovely Christmas,' Cassie said dreamily.

She told the boys everything, even about the king. 'I was only eight!' she said. It was more than four years ago. They had trusted each other absolutely, those two.

The three of them briefly considered the naivety of eight year olds. Adam returned to his sketchbook.

'When your uncle stopped being a spy,' Edward said, 'what did he do for a living?'

Cassie fidgeted. 'I think he translated things,' she said vaguely.

'Books?'

'No. Papers mostly, I think. I never asked him.'

It occurred to Cassie that she had handed Uncle Peter her daily experience like a meal on a plate and expected him to be interested in it all. But she'd shown no interest in his. Not the slightest! *I am a horrible selfish person*, she thought. This was an enduring fear of hers, which surfaced from time to time.

But there *had* been a book, she remembered, and she'd asked him about it. What sort of book is it? she'd demanded. A story book? Yes, he'd said. Something like that.

'What's it going to be called?'

'*War and Peace*,' he'd said – and she'd felt uneasy because she thought someone else had written a book with that title.

But after that he kept the book out of sight, hidden from her.

Adam, without raising his eyes from his drawing, said, 'Was there something *dangerous* about it? Something *secret*?'

'I don't know. I never looked at it.' *I was not*, she admitted sadly to herself, *sufficiently interested.*

Edward changed the subject. 'Why did you cycle to Ely?' he asked. 'After the funeral?'

'I was in a panic. I thought it would help if I talked to Dame Lily. She's my favourite teacher. Well, sort of.'

'*Dame* Lily? What's a *dame*?'

'Some kind of duchess, I think,' Cassie said vaguely.

'*Did* you talk to her?'

Cassie shook her head. 'The play was on. She was busy.'

Adam was still calmly drawing in his sketchbook. Cassie – self-conscious about her bare legs and preparing to be angry if he was drawing them – got up to have a look.

But it was her feet that Adam had drawn. Two bare feet, the toes of her right foot clenched over her left.

My feet! she thought. *Why would anyone draw my feet?*

There was a distant approaching roar, a great booming bass note in the heavens, growing louder. At first they paid it no attention. Planes were always passing overhead, on their way in or out of the airfield. But these sounded different.

'Bombers,' Adam said. '*Lots* of bombers!'

Edward sat up straight, Cassie cocked her head.

The sound was low and intensifying, coming closer. But there was a difference: the approach was slower and heavier, a deep and solid thunder rolling across the heavens towards them.

'There must be hundreds of them!'

They jumped to their feet and rushed outside. The bright late-evening sky seemed to be full of aircraft, a great sky-convoy of wide-winged bombers not yet in formation. They were still low after take-off, and each was towing a glider, the helmeted heads of the pilots clearly visible, almost as if you could speak to them. The gliders were fat-bellied and heavy. Their massive wingspans looked unstable, and their fuselages had a clumsy and squarish look about them, with fixed landing wheels sticking out awkwardly.

The deep roar in the sky shook the ground under their feet and made their hearts tremble. Edward felt a pang of fear, and wondered what it would be like to be on the other side as this great flying armada approached.

Its menace was palpable.

'Halifaxes!' Adam shouted.

'And Horsas!' Edward shouted back.

Cassie couldn't tell a Halifax from a Tiger Moth, so she said nothing.

'Heading south-west,' Edward said as the last of the planes flew out of sight beyond the treetops and the sound began to fade.

Back inside, they talked excitedly about what they'd seen. 'The beginning,' Edward said.

'The build-up,' Adam said with satisfaction. 'Any day now.'

Is this, Cassie thought, *how boys talk about the War? Without verbs? Without explanations?* 'What's the *point* of gliders?' she asked recklessly.

Edward was shocked by her ignorance. 'To land troops in advance of an invasion. So that they can capture enemy bridges and destroy guard posts.'

'They're enormous things,' Adam said dreamily. 'You can carry twenty or thirty men in each one. And some can carry artillery, or a tank.'

A *tank*? It seemed impossible, and Cassie was briefly silenced by disbelief.

'They're gathering,' Edward said. 'For the invasion.'

'It's got to be soon,' said Adam.

'*Why* has it?'

'Because the days are getting longer and the nights are shorter.'

'But they were flying south-west. That's the wrong direction,' Cassie said. 'Hitler's forces are concentrated near Calais, where the sea crossing is shortest.'

'How do you know that?' Adam said.

How *did* she know that? Cassie couldn't remember. She supposed Uncle Peter must have mentioned it. But she *did* know it – and neither of the boys did.

14
Uncle Peter's Book

Cassie's sadness about Uncle Peter seemed to have unaccountably disappeared, washed away by a wave of excitement. *But my uncle has just died*, she thought. *Surely I'm not allowed to be happy.*

Outside, Edward had seen Cassie's bike, and it had reminded him. 'What have you got in your saddlebag?' he asked.

'What? Nothing!' she said.

'I could feel the weight of it when I cycled back from Ely last night.'

Cassie frowned. She *never* kept anything in her saddlebag. 'There's nothing in it,' she said again. 'Absolutely nothing.'

'There must be!' Edward insisted.

All three raced to the door, ruthlessly shouldered each other to get through, and hurried round to the side of the guard's van where the bike was leaning.

The fasteners on Cassie's saddlebag were undone and hanging loose. Edward lifted the flap and stared. Cautiously he lifted something out.

'It's Uncle Peter's book!' Cassie's words came out with a strange little gasp, as if she couldn't breathe.

And what a book it was! – a massive volume; thick, tattered and dirty. It was bound in leather, its cover was scratched and scuffed. There had once been a picture of flowers there but half of this had been torn off. There were brown circular marks where someone had stood mugs of coffee or tea.

But if the outside of the book was strange, the contents inside defied understanding.

Every page was covered with Uncle Peter's tiny writing, all done with a sharpened pencil. On some pages his pencil sharpenings were still there, smeared and flattened into the paper – minute dusts of graphite and tiny flakes of wood. There were grease stains too, and squashed crumbs.

Some of the passages were several lines long, some were very short. Each one was dated – *twice*. In the left-hand margin one date would be written in blue ink, and on the right there was always another date written in red. The red date was mostly several days after the blue date.

It was baffling!

There were also newspaper cuttings pasted in, and they too were dated. Glued to the inside cover there was a folded road map of south-east England, covering East Anglia, the Thames estuary and Kent. This too had markings added in red, arrows from one place to another, and more dates.

All the arrows led south, towards the Kent coast, where Dover was – opposite Calais on the coast of enemy-occupied France.

'Let's go back inside,' Cassie said in a small voice. They felt all three, instinctively, that this baffling volume was dangerous and, above all, *secret*.

So they took it into the guard's van and sat on the bed, with Cassie in the middle. Six knees side by side, with the book on Cassie's lap.

'Was he trying to write some kind of story?' Adam said. 'A war story?'

'Not as far as I know,' Cassie said. She felt excited and jumpy, weirdly happy in fact. The book seemed to bring Uncle Peter back to life.

'This must have taken him *months*!' Edward said. 'But what is it *for*?'

The first page was dated 18th November 1943. And after that all the entries, both written and glued-in, were dated in chronological order. Most of the entries were short and sharp, written with words missed out, like telegrams. *Number Seven Tank Division delayed. ETA Wednesday*, one said. *Supreme Command concerned fuel supply to K23 insufficient.* Some seemed trivial, and almost out of place among such military messages: *Outbreak of chicken pox among Fifth Canadian Brigade. Vital every effort to isolate.*

There were characters whose names kept cropping up. One of them was *Grey Squirrel*, and beside one of his entries Uncle Peter had written something in red: *Return to this March 8th*. Then, when they looked ahead to March 8th thirty pages further on, there was another message from *Grey Squirrel*. There were lots of these links, each

81

correctly followed up. One message from *Grey Squirrel* said: *Ensure all major troop movements avoid centre of Canterbury*. There was an immediate reply reminding all staff not to mention places by name – and after that there was nothing else from *Grey Squirrel*. He was never mentioned again.

The newspaper cuttings were mostly concerned with troop movements in the countryside. One complained that an entire herd of milking cows had been terrified by an army convoy so long that it took all day to pass through the village. Another described how a tank from the US army had crashed into a pub in Kent, obstructing the road so that the 280 vehicles that were following had to make a detour through a farmyard. A vicar had written a letter to his local paper complaining that girls were being corrupted by a massive invasion of American soldiers. He'd seen one girl, he wrote in outrage, chewing gum in church.

On and on it went, a catalogue of incidents reported from inside and outside the military authorities. More than 300 pages of it.

'It's a kind of diary,' Edward said cautiously. He suspected it was against the law to write such a thing in a time of war.

It became even more baffling when they moved to the end of the book. For the dated items didn't stop when Uncle Peter had died. He had written them *into the future*. There were entries dated right through May and June, and ahead into the beginning of July.

'How could he know these things were going to happen?'

'He *must* have been writing a story,' Adam said. 'A novel – and this was his plan for it.'

Oh, Uncle Peter! Cassie thought. *What were you up to?*

'How did it get inside your saddlebag?' Edward asked.

'And *why* was it in your saddlebag?' Adam said.

Cassie closed the book with a thump and Edward studied the front cover more carefully. Adam's instinct was different. He liked clean empty paper, so he turned to the unused pages at the back. On one of them, insignificant in thin pencil, someone had written *Knightsbridge 700. JIC.*

Cassie's heart seemed to stop. *Uncle Peter is speaking to me from the dead*, she thought.

'It's a phone number,' Edward said. 'But who's J.I.C.?'

'It's not a person,' she said. 'It means *just in case*. It's a message to me.'

Her heart recovered and started to race wildly. Either Uncle Peter had hidden the book in a hurry, or he had left it for her to find. Or both. She was sure of it. *And* the telephone number. A troubling idea lodged itself in her mind – had he *known* he was going to die?

The two boys were waiting, and she knew the question they would put to her. '*Will* you phone?'

'Yes,' she said, looking from one to the other. 'I must.'

'There's a phone box on Fen Common,' Adam said.

'But we'll have to wait until after dark, in case you're seen.'

The boys rehearsed all manner of different things she might say when she phoned. And different ways of saying them. But they kept going back to Uncle Peter's book, and making new discoveries about the strange fictions it contained.

And Cassie? She was astonished (and ashamed) to find that she was still enjoying herself.

The supper that Edward brought was a good one. He and Cassie ate it greedily. Adam had only a small portion because he would have his main evening meal later. In a barn, Cassie thought he'd said.

A *barn*?

As darkness fell the prospect of making the phone call made her gloomy. She knew she ought to feel cheered; it was a clue, a sign for her to follow, a hint of help. But, instead, she was scared.

Pull yourself together! she said to herself. *You mustn't show you're scared. Mustn't worry your champion.*

When it was almost dark, they walked to the end of the lane and round to Fen Common, where the phone box stood, silent and shadowy. All three of them crowded in, elbow to elbow, shoulder to shoulder.

'Knightsbridge seven hundred, please,' Cassie said firmly. The boys watched her face in the darkness.

The coins fell into the machine, and Cassie listened

anxiously to the phone ringing at the other end. Then a voice sang out, 'You're through!'

A woman spoke. 'This is Knightsbridge seven hundred.'

They had considered and rehearsed the next bit, over and over. 'Can I speak to Uncle Peter, please?'

I am ringing up heaven, Cassie thought, *and asking to speak to a dead person.*

A pause. And, despite the distance, Cassie knew the speaker at the other end was thinking what to say. Then, 'One moment, please.'

Should my heart be beating as fast as this? Cassie thought.

A different speaker came on the line, a man. 'This is Caistor & Walkman. How can I help you?'

But it was suddenly too much for Cassie. She slammed down the receiver and pushed herself desperately out of the door as if she was unable to breathe, followed by the two puzzled boys. She turned her back on them and had nothing to say. She felt – absurdly – that she should apologise. They had expected more of her.

'Can we go back to your guard's van?' she said to Edward.

Abigail and Molly had been waiting in Paradise Barn for what seemed like ages. 'Where *is* he? He should have been here *hours* ago!'

At the back of the barn a wooden staircase led up to an unexpected room which the children had been allowed to use as their den for the last four years – since 1940 in fact, when Adam had arrived as an evacuee.

The girls had made everything ready. The fire was burning in the grate; a large saucepan full of cold baked beans waited to be heated up; a loaf of stale bread waited to be sliced and toasted; a brass toasting fork with Ely Cathedral on the handle leaned by the fire, ready for action; and the window was blacked out so that no enemy aircraft could spot the light of their candles.

They could not have made it more snug.

Outside it was completely dark. Inside, the girls grew restless. Abigail was irritable, Molly anxious. Both were hungry.

They heard a sound downstairs. Their half-hearted game of happy families was instantly forgotten as they strained their ears. Someone had come into the barn.

But this was not Adam. He would have called out to them. He always did that.

Molly picked up one of the candlesticks. 'Let's look,' she whispered.

'Not with a candle! We don't want to be seen until we know who's looking.'

They crept out onto the wooden platform at the top of the stairs. Crouching side by side, they peered down into the pitch-dark body of the barn.

Someone was walking slowly round the barn, apparently searching. The backlight from his torch lit up his face and shone weirdly on his glasses. He looked unhurried, unworried, and deeply, deeply sinister.

'It's that horrible little man who's staying at our guest house,' Molly whispered. 'With the thick specs.'

Mr Tittipat was systematic in his search. From the big door where he had entered, he moved round the barn in an anti-clockwise direction, slowly investigating every shadowy space behind the farm machinery that stood there. The steps that led up to the cabin were obscured by a gigantic threshing machine, but when he shone his light there he would inevitably see them.

Were they scared, these two girls, at the sight of this unpleasant man in his city suit calmly exploring their barn after dark? Well no, not really. They were roused and excited – certainly not frightened in the way they would have been a few years earlier. Molly was a tall strong girl, and Abigail almost as tall, and wiry too. Both were very capable, with a muscular confidence that they could deal with almost anything that Mr Tittipat could threaten them with.

– unless he had a gun. But Molly thought of that later, when it was over.

Mr Tittipat stopped moving. Unexpectedly, he shouted in a high voice, 'Come out! Come out from wherever you are!'

Nothing. A long intensified silence followed this nightmare cry, as if the ancient building had hushed itself to pay attention.

'Reveal yourself, child! I *shall* find you in the end.'

Then, suddenly, Mr Tittipat swung abruptly round to face the entrance. Someone was standing in the open doorway, silhouetted black against the plum-coloured darkness outside. 'It's Adam!' Molly whispered, no more loudly than a breath.

Adam took a couple of steps inside. 'Can I help you?' he said firmly.

'Don't be impertinent, young man!' Mr Tittipat said coolly. He sounded pleased, almost triumphant, as if he'd discovered something or solved a problem. 'What are you doing here? Shouldn't you be in bed, like other little boys?'

Adam walked right up to him. 'Mr Tottipot,' he said amiably, 'this is where I'm sleeping. So what are *you* doing here?'

'Sleeping here?' Mr Tittipat shone his torch directly into Adam's eyes.

'Please don't do that,' Adam said to him.

But Mr Tittipat held the torch steady – until Adam, in an uncharacteristic flash of anger, grabbed his wrist to turn it away. But the torch clattered to the ground and skidded across the brick floor with a small sound of breaking glass.

Everywhere was dark.

'You young fool! How am I supposed to find my way back without my torch?'

'I'll come with you if you like,' Adam said. He hadn't intended to break the torch.

'No thank you!'

Mr Tittipat stalked across the floor and left. And as Adam stood in the doorway Molly and Abigail almost flew down the stairs and across the barn to join him. They stood there, the three of them, crowding together in the darkness, to make sure that that hateful little man really had set off along the field path that led back to the town.

Joyfully the girls took Adam upstairs, the sin of his lateness forgotten and overlooked. *The three of us together*, Molly thought. The candles were relit, the coal on the fire was stirred to make a glowing red-hot place, the pan of beans was placed on it, a kettle of milk stood beside it for making cocoa, and the loaf was cut into twelve slices.

'Can we have eggs too?' Adam said.

But Abigail was firm. 'No, they're for breakfast. Tell us where you've been and why you were so late.'

Adam could be firm too. 'Not until we've had our

supper,' he said. 'I'm starving.' And because a large saucepan of baked beans takes a long time to heat up on an open fire, they got ready for bed, hustling and bustling companionably in the fluttering candlelight.

Then Abigail and Adam sat side by side on the bed in their bedclothes, and Molly knelt on the floor in hers, blissfully toasting slice after slice of bread at the fire, while they told each other again and again about Adam's triumph over Mr Tittipat. 'I suppose I'll have to buy him a new torch,' Adam grumbled.

'You'll have to say sorry too,' Abigail said.

Adam shrugged. Molly smiled a secret smile, knowing he was perfectly capable of *saying* sorry.

After they'd eaten the beans on toast and washed it down with cocoa, they blew out all but one of the candles and got into their beds. Molly had been thinking about this moment all week, enjoying it in anticipation.

'Now!' Abigail said to Adam. 'Where were you?'

'With young Edward,' he said. 'He wanted to show me something.'

'What?'

'Something he's found.'

'Adam! *What* has he found?'

'I guess,' Adam said slowly, 'that Edward has found what old Tattipit is looking for.'

Both girls sat up in bed and glared down at Adam where he lay on the floor, half in his sleeping bag, with his hands under his head.

'Only it's not a thing. It's a person. A girl.'

They'd both heard about the missing girl, of course. Everyone in Great Deeping knew about her. But that Edward had found her seemed amazing.

'She's in his railway carriage?' Molly asked in disbelief.

'It's a brake van,' Abigail said.

'Well, that's where she's hiding. And young Edward has been looking after her. Since yesterday.'

The story was gradually told and grasped, its every detail deliciously lingered over and savoured to the full. It was long after midnight when they exhausted this interesting topic. *Were they going to be part of this?* they wondered. *Should they join with Edward and offer their help?*

But Abigail was one step ahead. As she stretched to blow out the last candle she said, 'We're already part of it.'

'Why are we?'

'It's obvious! Because Mr Tippitup now thinks *we have the missing girl here.*'

It took another half hour to talk about what this might mean. But Abigail fell asleep after that, and soon there was silence in the cabin.

After a while a voice came out of the darkness. 'Did you draw her?'

'I drew her feet,' Adam said.

And later, when both girls were asleep, Adam

91

remembered that he'd forgotten to tell them about that book. Uncle Peter's mysterious book.

'A *boy?*' Cassie said. *'Dress like a boy?'* She looked
hopefully at Edward in search of a better idea. She'd
always been thankful *not* to have been born a boy.

'Well, you can't hide all the time,' Edward said
reasonably. 'And you can't go out dressed like that. But
if we could disguise you . . .'

Rain fell heavily onto the roof of the brake van. The
trees outside were black, gleaming with wet.

'Why can't I be disguised as a girl?' Cassie wailed.
But she knew the answer: in girls' clothes, she would
always be recognisable.

She stuck out her bottom lip in a pretend sulk. But
she said yes, all right. She supposed it would be a relief
to be able to go about freely. But how could it be done?

As they were finishing breakfast – two boiled eggs,
three slices of toast cut into soldiers, and a mug of milk
– they heard a clamour of voices in the trees outside.
It sounded like a class of children on a nature walk.

Instantly, Cassie backed away into a corner of the
brake van, on the bed with her knees drawn up tight.
How she wished she'd never put on those shorts!

The door of the wagon slid sideways and there was

Adam. Behind him two girls were pushing him in, shamelessly eager to get a look at the newcomer. They took off wet woolly hats and damp macs smelling of rain. With them was a little boy.

One of the girls, the taller of the two, said shyly, 'Hello.'

'How many people have you told about me?' Cassie said to Adam.

If she was angry, her anger was wasted on Adam. 'Just these three,' he said. 'And they won't tell anyone.'

I didn't expect you to tell anyone! Cassie thought.

'Don't be cross with Adam,' one of the girls said. 'He told us about you because we're friends and we tell each other everything. I'm Abigail, by the way, and this is Molly. And this is Molly's brother, William. He's four.'

Edward watched, looking worriedly from one to the other. Cassie pulled a cushion across her lap, covering her tight lemon shorts.

Abigail – who had spotted the empty eggshells – said cheerfully, '*We* had boiled eggs too.'

Then it all came out: that they had a room of their own in a barn, that Molly's mum owned a guest house, and that one of the guests staying there (called Tittipat) had turned up in their barn the previous night, clearly looking for someone.

'Who was he looking for?' Edward asked.

Wasn't it obvious? '*Her!*' Abigail said. 'Cassie.'

'How do you know that?'

'Who else could it be?'

'What's he like, this Mister What's-his-name?'

Slowly it began to make sense. Mr Tittipat had arrived before Uncle Peter's funeral, and he was looking for someone. 'He thinks we're hiding you in our barn,' Adam said. And when Molly described what he looked like, Cassie knew at once that he'd been one of the men following her at the open-air theatre.

'So you might as well start liking us,' Abigail said cheerfully, 'because we're in this now whether you want us or not. *And* we can keep a secret.'

'What about . . . ?' Cassie looked at William, who looked gravely back at her, saying nothing.

'William is the best secret-keeper of all,' Abigail said.

Cassie was warming to them in spite of herself. 'Why do you live in a barn?' she said. *And why*, she added in her head, *does the one called Molly keep looking at my feet? Are they all foot mad?*

'We don't *live* in a barn . . .' Slowly the complicated realities of these new lives became clearer to her and – not for the first time – Cassie wondered how she could have lived in the same town as these people and known nothing at all about their existence. *Where* was *I all that time?* she wondered. *What* was *I doing?*

'*I* know where we've seen you!' Molly said, suddenly realising. 'On the school bus – you're the girl in the purple uniform! You go to St Dorothea's.'

Cassie nodded emphatically. 'That's me,' she said.

'*And* we've seen you at the cinema.'

'Yes. I love going to the pictures!'

And Abigail said, 'Do you go a lot?'

'Yup! Best place in the world! Practically live there.'

Abigail brought them back to the present. 'Well, what are we going to do?'

'Edward thinks I should disguise myself,' Cassie said. She sounded haughty, as if the idea was ridiculous.

'Well, you certainly can't go anywhere dressed like that,' Abigail said.

'– as a *boy*!' Cassie added, less haughtily this time. 'Only we haven't got any boys' clothes, not big enough anyway.'

Edward felt he had to say the sensible thing. 'Don't you think we ought to tell the police?' he said. This wasn't what he wanted. It would come to an end and Cassie would be taken away.

'Ah,' Adam said. 'I don't think we can do that . . .'

That morning Adam had cycled across the town to Uncle Peter's house. He'd leaned his bike against the garden wall and boldly approached the front door. He rang the front doorbell, and knocked, getting no response. Then he stepped onto the lawn and peered into the front window.

But the house told him nothing. It was full of phenomena but empty of evidence. There was nothing in it to indicate that the house's owner had recently died, or explain why Cassie had found strangers inside.

He straightened up sharply when he heard footsteps approaching from the street. It was a policeman, homely and unhurried, wearing a black cape against the rain –

Constable Simpson, a familiar and friendly sight to everyone in Great Deeping for the last twenty-five years.

'And what do you think you're up to, young man?'

Adam had prepared for that question. 'I'm looking for Cassie,' he said.

'And why would you be wanting her?'

'We're friends.'

'You know about her uncle?'

'Yes. But I thought perhaps . . .'

Constable Simpson was a soft touch where children were concerned. 'Well she won't be seeing her friends for a long time!' he said. 'She's gone away.' And because he could see no harm in it, he went on to tell Adam that Cassie had gone to Leeds. To live with a great-aunt, or someone like that. For good.

'So you see,' Adam said to them. 'There's no point in telling the police. They're telling lies about you anyway.'

Molly couldn't bring herself to believe such a thing. 'They wouldn't,' she said.

Abigail was more cynical. 'Perhaps someone high up has *ordered* them to say that.'

Cassie sat forward on the bed, tightly clutching her knees as if she needed to hold her body parts together. *Here I am*, she thought ruefully, *body and bones, mind and muscle, here, in Deeping. Me – just as real as I've ever been! Yet officially I am in Leeds!*

'Are you all right?' Molly asked her.

'Absolutely!' Cassie said. And then she thought: *why* shouldn't *she become a boy?*

Molly, it turned out, knew where a supply of boys' clothes could be found. The previous year an old man had brought his grandson on a fishing holiday and they had stayed at her mum's guest house. At the end of their stay, they had left behind a suitcase full of the boy's clothes. There had been no reply to Mrs Barnes' letter about it.

'And Adam is about the right size,' Edward said. 'Perhaps he has one or two things . . .'

'He has one of everything to wear and one for the wash,' Molly said. 'And nothing to spare.'

Everyone laughed, including Adam. 'That's more than I've got,' Cassie said – and everyone laughed again.

17
Three Bags of Sand

Throughout the months of spring and early summer the country waited like a single watchful organism with a million eyes.

Everyone was so *tired*, so weary of this War! It had dragged on now for almost five years! People wondered if it was ever going to end.

Yet, in spite of everything, people took the train and visited grandma for her sixtieth birthday; they stood in cramped kitchens bottling plums, or making jam, pickles, and dried eggs; they plotted a Labour government for after the War so that you wouldn't have to pay to see a doctor; they went on day trips to the seaside where, as likely as not, you couldn't go far into the water because there were coils of barbed wire in case the enemy invaded; they went to dances in the village hall, or sang gaily along with music on the BBC Forces Programme; they spent long evenings on quiet allotments; they sat in draughty outside toilets and thought how nice it would be to have a lavatory indoors; they went on Sundays to quiet cemeteries to put flowers on graves.

Seventeen-year-old boys counted the days to their

next birthday, when they'd be called up for military service.

But they never stopped paying attention. With a million eyes they saw that something new was going on. They saw the massive movements of thousands of troops – British, Canadian and American mostly. Long convoys of army trucks towing guns rumbled along country roads. Whole trains, filled with soldiers, snaked their way along the country's railways. Tanks were to be seen everywhere – chewing up road surfaces, or carried on flat-bed railway wagons, or behind lorries so huge that children in villages stood gazing in awe, and the soldiers driving the trucks looked loftily down as they passed.

They went in all directions. But the general movement was *south* and *west*, in a mysterious drawing together of military determination, a focusing of purpose. The million-eyed British public knew that something was afoot. They did not know *where* precisely. They did not know *when* at all. But there was a quiet bracing of spirits.

At last!

When Hilda began chatting with the policeman on duty outside Mr Dinsdale's house she knew at once that it was hopeless. 'No, miss,' he said. 'Sorry! But I can't allow you to snoop around.'

'Oh, well,' she said sadly. 'I only wanted a peek. I say, it's jolly mizz for you having to stand here in the rain!'

He was unmoved by her sympathy. 'You a reporter?' he asked. 'Someone from the press?'

'Gosh, no! Just someone who's nosy! I'll go and have a look at your church instead. It's supposed to be very interesting. Can you give me some directions, please?' She gave him her sweetest smile.

A public footpath ran beside the Dinsdale house and he told her to go down there and across the sports field at the back. 'But mind you don't walk on the cricket pitch!' he added sternly.

Hilda stood her bike against the curb and set off along the footpath between tall wooden fences streaked black with wet. When she reached the end she could see the church on the other side of the sports field. She made a beeline for it, resolutely walking across the cricket pitch and half expecting to hear the policeman bellowing at her. But the only sound in the world was the soft relentless hiss of the rain falling on the grass.

She spent about fifteen minutes inside the church and another two inspecting the rain-sodden wreathes on Peter Dinsdale's freshly filled-in grave. There was no gravestone yet, just a man-sized mound of earth loosely covered with squares of turf like bits of carpet.

She set off back across the sports field but this time she did not return to the footpath. She went to the gate at the bottom of the back garden, peering cautiously around in case there was another copper on duty there.

But there was no one, and Hilda snicked up the latch and stepped cautiously into the garden. There were no flower beds, just a lot of grass and a few very old fruit trees. Not very promising, she thought, but she was determined to examine as much as she could. She might even be able to get close enough to the house to peer in through the back windows.

There was a tree house in the largest of the fruit trees, with a ladder, and Hilda went hopefully across to investigate. She climbed four or five steps up the ladder until her face emerged above the floor. But she saw at once that the missing schoolgirl had clearly grown out of the tree house years ago. It was wet, abandoned and empty.

There was a wooden shed too, and that proved just as disappointing. Nothing there but some dismal garden tools. But behind the shed – in the narrow space between it and the hedge – she found something that didn't fit. Everything in Peter Dinsdale's back garden was dreary, shabby and old. But behind the shed – along with damp flower pots and old garden canes – there was something new and pristine, something that had not had time to take on the dull colouring of disuse. It was a folded bundle of freshly new hessian sacks. Three of them. They were like the sacks that millers and farmers used for storing grain, but she found when she picked them up that these had been used for carrying sand.

Sand?

One of the sacks had a piece of paper attached to it with a safety pin. It was a delivery note and, although the rain had made the ink run, the writing was still legible. *To Mr Dinsdale: builder's sand – 12-stone.* It was dated on the day after Mr Dinsdale had died. The supplier's name was printed at the top: *Broadbent Bros, Ltd, Station Road, Great Deeping.*

Hilda detached the delivery note and went inside the shed to consider it in the dry. Then, puzzled and thoughtful, she left by the back gate and returned to the front by the public footpath.

'Very lovely, your church!' she said to the policeman.

He grunted. 'Wouldn't know. I'm chapel. I hope you didn't walk across the cricket pitch.'

'Gosh, no!' Hilda said piously. 'That wouldn't do at all! This Dinsdale chappie – did you know him?'

'Yes, I did. Most people knew him. He was very well liked round here.'

'Someone told me,' Hilda said, 'that he was a practical man. Liked doing bits of building, plastering, that sort of thing.'

The policeman showed signs that he'd had enough of Hilda's questions, so she hastily changed direction. 'Mister Churchill builds walls – did you know? Bricklaying helps him to keep calm when he's troubled.'

The policeman admired Winston Churchill. 'No, I didn't know that,' he said. 'But Peter Dinsdale, *he* wouldn't know one end of a builder's trowel from the other! He hardly even bothered to touch his garden tools. No, the only tools he was any good with were his pen and his typewriter.'

So why, Hilda thought, was twelve-stone of builder's sand delivered to his house? And what had the sand been used for?

Ten minutes later Hilda rode her bike into the yard of the Broadbent brothers. 'This bally rain!' she said crossly to herself as she dismounted.

Along one side there was a large open-ended building with a great sagging roof. There were stacks of bricks, piles of timber, a tractor and cart, a smell of sawdust – and two men seated by a small table, dolefully watching the rain.

Doug and Willy Broadbent had served in World War One but were too old to serve in this one. There was so little work for them to do because of the War that they spent a lot of their time waiting. So they were both openly and unashamedly pleased to see a pretty young woman, even if she was soaked and cross.

Hilda walked towards them, taking off her woolly hat and shaking the rain out of it with an expression of disgust on her face.

'Come you in out of the wet!' Doug said.

'Have a mug of tea!' added Willy.

'Don't mind if I do!' Hilda said. She warmed to these two immediately.

A mug had to be found, and a stool for Hilda to sit on. The big black kettle had to be filled afresh and set to boil on an ancient gas ring. Only then were the two men ready to do business. 'What can we do for you?' Doug said.

'Sand!' Hilda said decisively. 'I need your advice about sand.'

She saw their disappointment, their feeling of being slightly let down. And she understood it, and sympathised – there was no money in advice. Selling was what they needed to do. However, they had invited her to take tea with them and they were too gallant to be unkind or discourteous.

'My grandmother – I say, it's jolly good to be out of that rain! – my granny lives out in Little Green, and she wants to lay a garden path. She's got some old paving stones but she asked me to find out about sand to lay them on. I'm visiting her, you see, and I know nothing about this sort of thing.'

For once, Hilda was not play-acting. She really knew nothing about laying paths. 'How do I order sand?' she said. 'By volume? By weight? Or what?'

'Well,' Willy Broadbent said slowly, 'you can order by volume, cubic yards. But most people just order a cartload and we generally know what they want. But the best thing is to order it by weight.'

'So I should work out how much sand I want by the stone?' she asked.

'Stone? No! *Hundredweight*, that's what we generally deal in.'

'So people don't order sand by the stone?' Hilda said cautiously.

'Not usually,' Doug said. He seemed to have closed down that line of conversation, but his brother chipped in. 'Well, we did have one order recently. You remember, Doug, that order for Peter Dinsdale. That was an order for twelve-stone of sand.'

'So it was,' said Doug, remembering.

'I thought he'd died,' Hilda said casually.

'Well, that's the strange thing,' Willy said in a lowered voice suitable for discussing death.

'Milk?' Doug asked. Hilda nodded.

'Someone placed that order by phone the morning *after* he died. Now why would he want builders' sand when he was dead? And two days later we were paid by cheque – and the postmark on the envelope was somewhere in London.'

'Sugar?'

'No thanks,' Hilda said. 'I have to watch my weight.'

She said it without thinking. She was still preoccupied with sand. And when the two brothers started joking about *her* slimness and *their* fatness, she was irritated by the distraction – until one of them said, 'Sixteen stone I weighed last summer! We went on a day trip to Hunstanton, y'know, and I weighed myself on one of them machines. Sixteen stone! I couldn't believe it! But my brother – *he* only weighs twelve. Skinny little thing he is! Twelve stone!'

'She went as white as a sheet when I said that,' Doug said to Willy afterwards. 'Now how do you account for that?'

Hilda cycled furiously back into town in search of a phone box.

Her hands shook with rage as she searched for pennies in her purse. But she found what she wanted and in a few minutes she was speaking to Group Captain Rayburn.

'Hilda? Is that you?'

'Shut up and pay attention! I'm bloody angry! Now, you get in touch with Mr Pinstriped Suit from Secret Ops and get him back down here for nine o'clock tomorrow morning! I have a few things I want to say to him!'

'How dare you speak to me in that tone!' the group captain retorted. 'I can't give him orders. You know that.'

'Get him here,' Hilda snapped. 'Tell him, if he isn't here tomorrow morning, I'll blow the whole damn thing sky high!'

'What are you talking about?' Group Captain Rayburn sounded scared.

'I mean it!' Hilda said. 'Do as I say.' She slammed the receiver back onto its holder.

Who would have thought that a change of clothes and a haircut could be so bracing?

In the suitcase that Molly brought there were shirts, vests, pants, trousers, socks, a mackintosh and two woollen jerseys. And a precious pair of brown shoes that fitted Cassie perfectly, along with a pair of boys' sandals.

'But what about my . . . ?' Cassie said, fluttering her hands in front of her chest, and with one of her lowered sidelong looks.

'Wear something loose,' Molly said.

The rain had stopped at last, and the boys went out into the warm sun while the girls stayed inside to help with Cassie's transformation. When at last she came out onto the platform at the end of the brake van – with Molly and Abigail behind her – the person they stared at was certainly *not* a boy.

It was not just her hair (which still had to be dealt with) – it was her legs. Despite the grey socks and the brown shoes they were still unmistakably the legs of a girl. No one would be deceived.

Adam reached for his sketchbook. 'Don't you dare, Adam Swales!' Abigail said.

They took Cassie back into the brake van, and she came out again wearing a pair of grey flannel trousers. *Long* trousers.

Uncle Peter had told her that if you were in disguise you had to *become* the person you were trying to look like. 'But I just feel naked inside somebody else's clothes,' Cassie said.

'We're all naked inside our clothes,' Abigail pointed out.

However, the long trousers were a big improvement.

Her hair had to be dealt with next. Ruefully she handed the scissors to Edward and sat herself down on a fallen tree trunk in the dappled afternoon sun.

He stood behind her, gently lifting trusses of her dark-brown hair. He didn't know whether he loved or hated the soft crunch of the blades as they sliced through. The others chipped in from time to time with advice, but he ignored all of it. Slowly the back of Cassie's neck appeared, and there was a harvest of brown hair on the wet grass at his feet. 'How long will it take to grow again?' he asked.

'Years!' Cassie said mournfully. It felt to Molly that what they'd done was irreversible, and mysteriously full of meaning. A private shiver ran up her spine.

Then it was Abigail's turn. She had brought from home a pair of hand clippers ('My mum used to cut my dad's hair,' she explained). Taking Edward's place she used the clippers to taper the hair around Cassie's ears and down the back of her neck. Edward watched, absorbed and regretful, as the soft tender curls he had uncovered at the nape of her neck were shorn off.

It was the final stage of a boy's short back and sides. Cassie stood up slowly, running her hand over her shorn head and neck. 'How does it feel?' Adam asked.

'Draughty!' Cassie said. She laughed uncertainly, feeling an illogical rush of affection for these new friends. 'Now I need a new name,' she said.

'Anthony Cassell,' Molly said at once. She'd been thinking about it ever since the idea of disguise had come up. 'Because if anyone hears us call you Cassie by mistake, we can say it's short for Cassell.'

Everyone thought that was rather clever. 'But what are we going to do now?' Abigail said.

'Can I see your barn?' Anthony Cassell said.

Disguise takes time to get accustomed to. So, when three boys, two girls and a four-year-old toddler larked their way across town that afternoon, one of them was wary, casting sidelong glances at every passer-by.

No one would be deceived, Cassie thought.

But she found herself walking slightly differently, as if the boys' shoes and the long trousers were directing her shoulders to lean forward a little and swing slightly from side to side. What's more, she felt unaccountably *happy*. She had never – never! – walked the streets with a group of friends.

They took Molly's brother home for his dinner.

Then, back in the street, Edward said, 'I've been wondering . . .'

But *should* he speak? Was it wise to raise her hopes only to have them dashed if he were wrong? And yet he had a theory, and he thought he should tell them about it.

'Why do you think Dame Lily didn't go to your uncle's funeral?' he said cautiously.

'Because she didn't like him as much as he liked her,' Cassie said sharply. They shot out, those words, as if they'd been in hiding, waiting for the chance.

'Because she was busy with her play?' Abigail suggested.

'Why, young Edward?' Adam said. 'Have you got an idea?'

'It's just possible,' Edward said, 'that she didn't go because he isn't dead – and she knows he isn't.'

That stopped them in their tracks and they gathered in a close-huddled group, pretending to study the contents of a sweet-shop window. It was a bizarre idea. Crazy!

'Well, she was supposed to be Uncle Peter's friend.' (*More* than a friend, Cassie thought.) 'And friends usually go to each other's funerals.'

And Abigail said, 'Only the ones left alive do that. The dead ones can't!'

'Dead people do go to their own funerals,' Molly said quietly.

'Perhaps Cassie's Uncle Peter didn't,' Adam said.

'Dame Lily didn't look very sad when I saw her backstage.' Cassie, staring at her reflection in the window, thought suspiciously about Dame Lily with one part of her mind, and marvelled at her boy-reflection with another.

'There you are then!' Abigail said, as if that proved it.

'But how could he *not* be dead?' Cassie said. 'They buried him.' She was in earnest now. This was serious. The undertaker, the coffin, the grave, Miss Jardine breaking the news to her – could it be that the whole grim sequence could be unpicked and explained differently?

'They buried a coffin,' Edward said. 'But you don't know if your Uncle Peter was in it.'

Adam, seized by mischief, began solemnly:

'It wasn't the *cough*

That carried him *off*,

'Twas the *coff*in

They carried him *off* in.'

And the others joined in, chanting in time as they goose-stepped along the street. 'It wasn't the *cough* that carried him *off* . . .'

Cassie joined in too. *I'm going crazy*, she thought.

But the craziness quickly petered out. 'Old Mr Ross would have known if there wasn't a body in the coffin,' Abigail pointed out. 'He would have *said*!'

Cassie stopped dead, suddenly alert, all craziness gone. 'But it *wasn't* Mr Ross!' she said. 'It was an undertaker from London.'

They were startled by this. It changed everything. And Edward – amazed at himself – invented an entire plot in an instant. 'Suppose your uncle needed to disappear for some reason. What better way could there be than to arrange his own death? He had to use a different undertaker because old Mr Ross wouldn't have kept it secret.'

'But how . . . ?'

'He used to be a spy. You *said*. So he would have been good at disappearing.'

This was too much for Cassie. 'If Uncle Peter had wanted to disappear he would have *told* me. *He told me everything!*' Why did she have to keep on telling them that? Why wouldn't they believe her?

'Perhaps there wasn't time to tell you,' Edward said.

Could that be it? 'But if he had time to arrange a funeral,' she said, 'he would have had time to tell me about it!'

Abigail chipped in cheerfully. 'There's another possibility,' she said. 'Perhaps *someone else* wanted him to disappear.'

Edward's idea, and Abigail's grim variation of it, took root in the no-man's land between reality and play. Probably none of them actually believed either version. But what if Edward was right? Or Abigail? So they held in their minds two contradictory things – just as Edward fully understood that his long-dead father would *not* show up one day alive and rescued.

But what if he did?

Mr Tittipat did not conduct his investigations from the guest house. He arranged with Mr Cheadle to rent a small office on the top floor of the solicitor's premises in the High Street, where there was a telephone with its own number so that he could contact the outside world without having to go through Mr Cheadle's receptionist downstairs. He could tell just by looking at her that she would have listened in on his conversations.

He did not make his own enquiries. He had a team of people whose task it was to gather information. One of them would make a small discovery which on its own seemed to be of no significance. But Mr Tittipat had *all* the pieces of information; only he could see the pattern they made.

The people of Great Deeping were unaware that there were several investigators in their midst. Consider the ants, Mr Tittipat had once said to his aged mother. If a few of them attempt to enter an alien ant heap, the resident ants fall upon the intruders and tear them to pieces. Mr Tittipat's team, however, was so well trained that not only did their hosts *not* tear them apart but they hardly noticed they were there.

The only female member of his team phoned Mr Tittipat that morning. 'Sir? I went to investigate the barn, sir. As you instructed.'

She paused for her commander to show some interest, give some response. But he simply waited.

'Three children are camping there, sir. One of them is the daughter from where you're staying, sir. And their evacuee – a boy called Adam Swales – is another. Then there's another girl, a girl called Abigail Murfitt.'

Mr Tittipat sighed. He knew that already. It was part of his pattern.

'I don't think they have any connection with our investigation, sir. But . . .'

'Out with it, you stupid woman! *What?*'

'Something went wrong, sir.'

Mr Tittipat showed no more interest than if he'd observed a wasp alight on a baby's bare arm.

'They had set a trap, sir.'

'*Someone's been here!*'

They'd crowded up the stairs, eager to show Cassie their room in the barn. But as they burst in Abigail stopped them. 'Someone's been here. *Look!*'

When they were younger – and because there was no lock on the cabin door – they had devised a trap to show them if an intruder had been there. There was a small bookshelf loosely fixed to the wall by screws that were too small for their holes. Adam had found a large diary with *Private* on the spine, and solidly glued its entire cover to one end of the shelf. It protruded slightly as if it had been hurriedly put back in place.

Next to it were seven other books.

They believed that any spies prowling about in their

room would not be able to resist taking down a book labelled *Private*. But they would have to pull it firmly, and in doing so they would pull away the whole shelf. The two loose screws and the other seven books would fall out. The shelf could be put back and the books replaced – but only an exceptionally careful intruder would have memorised the order in which the books had been arranged. It was not random, and it was not alphabetical. The books were placed according to the number of words in the title. *Ivanhoe* was the first, *Biggles Defies the Swastika* the fourth, and so on.

Molly had never been very interested in this invention, Adam rarely thought about it any more. But Abigail always checked it as soon as she entered the room. Now, as she pointed out, the shelf was in its proper position and the books were in place – *but not in the right order*.

'We were just *kids* when we thought about that,' she declared. 'But it *worked*!' She was excited by their own cleverness.

It all had to be explained to Cassie and Edward. It must be Tottipot, they thought first. Who else would go prowling around like that?

'Looking for me?' Cassie said.

It was scary, no doubt about it. But Molly pointed out that Mr Tittipat would have found no sign of Cassie in the barn. 'It's *good* that he's been here,' she said. 'He now thinks we're nothing to do with you. He won't bother with this place any more. Or us.'

After a time, Cassie began to feel reassured.

19
The Long Afternoon

Cassie hadn't known that you could spend an afternoon like that. In Uncle Peter's house – always alone – she would plan and decide what she was going to do until teatime, or supper time. Then she would do it, without deviating. But her new friends winged their way through the long warm afternoon, improvising and squabbling, playing a sudden game of tag among the farm machinery, then football outside against the wall, and finally a totally childish hide-and-seek back inside.

Everyone cheated cheerfully. And all these activities were so *physical* – shockingly physical to Cassie. Arms were grabbed, shirt-tails yanked out, eyes blindfolded by a pair of hands from behind. No allowance was made for Edward, who was smaller and younger; nor did he seem to need any. The wildest of all were Adam and Abigail, both of whom were ruthless and would do whatever was needed to get the ball, or find the best hiding place.

They were strong, these young people. And Cassie found she was strong too. When Adam hauled her bodily from behind a tractor tyre because he wanted to hide there himself, she grabbed him by his ankles and pulled him just as hard. Adam got a grip on the tyre so that it fell on top of him. Cassie's blood ran cold because she thought it had squashed him, but he squirmed free and just laughed.

Then – unaccountably and without anyone suggesting it – they all trooped upstairs and settled down quietly with ginger beer and biscuits.

Dusty and dishevelled, sweaty and breathless, they each found a place to sit. Two at the table, three on the bed. Edward sat beside Cassie, glancing with secret pleasure at the soft coppery-bronze hair on her bare arms in the warm sunlight; and her hands crossed on her lap, with grubby sensible fingers. *I wish I could draw like Adam,* he thought.

And Cassie was secretly thinking: *I like this place!* She'd never had such fun in her life. *I would like to sleep here*, she thought. *There's room for another sleeping bag.* But Edward would be hurt – and she wouldn't be disloyal to her half-hero.

Molly, saying little and thinking much, studied their new friend – the watchful eyes and her air of guardedness. *As if she were in a strange country and speaking a new language*, Molly thought. But you would *expect* a girl in her situation to be guarded! *And that's what eyes were for*, Molly thought, *to watch*.

'Tell us all about you,' Abigail said to Cassie.

But what was there to tell? Cassie pulled a comical face and stuck out her bottom lip. All those years she had been quietly happy with Uncle Peter – but she had never done anything worth telling. She read a lot of books, went to the pictures, did jigsaw puzzles, played Patience (*Im*patience, in her case). But she'd been nowhere, she realised, and seen nothing.

'Friends then?' Abigail said. 'Who are your friends?'

But she had no friends, Cassie confessed. 'At school, I am a day girl. Almost everyone else is a boarder.'

'Well, we'll be your friends now,' Abigail said.

As easily as that? Cassie wondered. *Was that how people became friends?* She looked at Molly, who caught her glance and smiled. 'Abso-bloomin-lutely!' Molly said.

They would be good friends to have, Cassie thought. But they were older than she was, and – she suspected – so joined-at-the-hip that she could never be a special friend to either of them.

Adam found his pencil and sketchbook. The others took no notice of this. They were used to it. Molly could see that Cassie wanted to move so that she could watch. *But she's too shy*, Molly thought.

'Do your parents let you stay here at night?' she said. This amazed her.

Abigail explained. 'My mum thinks two girls will be safe as long as *Adam* is with us. And Molly's mum thinks she and Adam will be safe as long as *I* am with them.'

'What are you going to do, now that you're disguised as a boy?' she asked later. 'Because we want to help. That's what friends are for.'

119

Cassie took a deep breath. 'Well, if Edward's right that my Uncle Peter isn't dead, I want to find him. Obviously!' But *should* she cling to Edward's idea?

'Then we need a plan,' Abigail said.

'Where are you going to stay?' Molly asked.

'In Edward's railway van, I hope,' Cassie said, looking at Edward for approval. Not for the world would she let him know that she'd rather live in the barn.

Edward nodded emphatically.

'Where are your dads?' Cassie asked them later.

Molly hated this question for Abigail's sake. 'Mine's in the army,' she said. 'In Italy.'

Quickly Abigail chipped in about hers. 'My dad is *missing feared dead*,' she said. She had explained this so many times that the words had become drained of sadness. They were just words that you had to say sometimes.

'Edward's dad is dead,' Adam said. 'And mine's in the London fire brigade.'

'This is the Land of Lost Fathers,' Cassie said melodramatically. *And uncles*, Molly thought, but she had the sense not to say it.

The two girls had heard only Adam's summarised account of Uncle Peter's funeral. So they made Cassie tell the whole story again, from the moment she'd run out of the church. 'I suppose those intruders were looking for Uncle Peter's book,' she said. 'At the time I was too scared to think clearly.'

'*What* book?'

The girls had never been told about Uncle Peter's book because Adam had forgotten about it. So, with difficulty and some help from Edward, Cassie described it.

'Was he writing a story?' Abigail said.

Cassie shook her head, troubled again by this baffling object. 'The things in it aren't true,' she said, 'but they might have been.'

'You mean he described things that hadn't happened?'

'Yes, but it's more complicated than that. He described things *in the future*. On February the first he wrote about something that would happen on the fifteenth! Only what he wrote about *didn't happen*!'

'Where is the book now?'

'In my brake van,' Edward said. 'I've disguised it,' he added proudly.

'We still haven't decided what we're going to *do*!' Abigail said. 'This is an investigation – so how are we going to *start*?'

Cassie said slowly, 'I'd like to get inside my house and have a proper look round. But I'm too scared to do it on my own.'

Molly liked her for admitting that. 'Isn't there a policeman guarding it all the time?' she said.

'We could distract him,' Adam said.

There was another of those group mood changes. Suddenly they were all energy and agreement. And – after a lot of eager suggesting and shouting each other down – they agreed on a plan of action. The only doubter was Edward. He thought they'd all gone out of their minds – but he stayed silent because he was the youngest. And because he didn't want to appear less brave than they were.

'Tomorrow then!' Abigail said.

'But there's another thing,' Adam said as he put away his pencils. 'You phoned that number and asked for Uncle Peter. Yesterday!'

She nodded. What was he getting at?

'The people you phoned will know which phone box you phoned from.'

Everyone stared at him. *So?*

'Well,' he said, 'they'll have set someone to watch it.'

Stunned silence. 'In case I go there again?' Cassie said in a small voice. She hated the thought of being *watched*, of people searching for her. It *scared* her.

'Well, let's go and find out then,' Abigail said, as if it were the most obvious thing in the world. And suddenly it was all bustle and rush again, as they tore down the stairs, across the barn and out into the afternoon sun.

20
The Watcher

Fen Common was full of the flash and brightness of early summer. In winter it was boggy, with low-level floods hidden in the long grass. But the rain had cleared and on a sunny day in May it was heaven! A donkey was tied up in a far corner close to its owner's cottage, there were seven tethered goats, along with chickens and a flock of ducks with vertical necks playing a frantic game of follow my leader.

The five friends established a space for themselves close to the telephone box at the roadside. Here they started a game of rounders, all the time keeping watch on the area around the phone box in search of someone on duty, someone waiting to pounce on a missing schoolgirl.

They saw no one.

Time passed, and still they saw no one.

Eventually they grew weary of rounders and gathered at a fallen tree trunk that acted as a seat.

Nearby there was a group of younger children. Most of them were probably seven or eight years old, some were as young as three or four, tagging along. There had been a good deal of shouting but now they lined up beside a shallow stream, and a sudden quiet descended on them.

A girl who went to Abigail's Sunday School saw her and shouted across. 'We're playing invasions!' Her face was flushed with excitement. 'We're the Second Front!'

About half the children were fighter planes, with wings outstretched and making loud humming noises as they stooped and sped across the grass. Bombers moved in a more stately manner, zooming low. One girl was attached by a piece of string to her brother's trouser-belt; she was a glider being towed. The other half were the army.

Shoes and socks were taken off and the Second Front splashed across the English Channel. Some held pretend binoculars to their eyes and scanned the far horizon. A submarine flung himself recklessly into the chilly water and lay there face down. The army came ashore with machine guns pointed and rat-tat-tatting from side to side. The bombers stooped low and made roaring noises like exploding bombs. The fighter planes turned into paratroopers, with their hands clasped above their heads and swaying from side to side until they landed. Then they too became machine gunners. The glider couldn't get herself untied and was still attached when the victorious advance was over.

Panting and triumphant, with wet feet, they cheered joyously. 'We've beaten the Germans!' their leader shouted. 'I'm Mr Churchill,' she explained to Abigail.

Adam, Molly and Abigail had played games like that

themselves when younger. So had Edward, but alone and inside his head. But Cassie never had. 'They missed out France,' she said. 'And Mr Churchill wouldn't lead the invasion himself.'

'Let's do it again!' one of the smaller ones shouted.

'But you haven't got an enemy,' Adam pointed out.

They looked slightly embarrassed by that – until Adam said, 'I'll be the enemy. *I'm Hitler!*' He jumped to his feet, put his left forefinger across his upper lip (for Hitler's moustache) and shot his right arm up and out. '*Heil Hitler!*' he shouted.

At this, they all screamed and returned to the far side of the ocean before lining themselves up and repeating the sea crossing. Again, the bombers droned, the fighter planes zoomed, the paratroopers jumped, and the glider, having got herself free at last, decided to go it alone and be a soldier wading ashore. There was more rat-tatting of machine guns, more roaring of bombs, and Adam disappeared under a triumphant and screaming allied army.

At last they all sobered down, went in search of shoes and socks, and fell quiet – except for the submarine, who was taking his trousers off because he was afraid there might be tadpoles in them.

'Go home, Sammy Norman,' Abigail said. 'You need to get those wet clothes off.'

When the youngsters had gone and the common was quiet, two extraordinary things happened.

First, the phone in the telephone box began to ring.

Now there's no reason why such a phone should not ring. It was connected to the network just like the phone in anyone's house. But it was troubling: somewhere in Britain an unknown person was ringing an empty phone box? *Why?*

The five children stared – and then the second amazing thing happened. Behind the phone box there was a ditch, with last year's tall feathery grey reeds and an occasional leaning willow.

One of these trees *gave birth to a man*. One moment he'd not been there. Then he was there. It was like a brilliant conjuring trick – and they all saw it.

None of them recognised the man and he seemed uninterested in them. He went into the phone box and picked up the phone. They all watched as he talked briefly, hung up, left the box, and walked off towards the centre of town.

What had seemed like a game (except to Cassie) was a game no longer. They were caught up in something real.

It is a hateful thing to be spied on.

'It *must* be a kind of story,' Molly insisted.

Inside Edward's railway van in the long fading light of evening, they were drawn to Uncle Peter's mysterious book as if it possessed a sinister magnetic power.

'He must have been planning to write a story about the War. And these are his ideas,' Molly said. She hoped she was right. Stories were safer.

'But why the dates?' Abigail grumbled. 'Why have *two* dates for every paragraph?'

Molly, who often wrote stories, thought that the first date indicated when he'd done the writing.

'I don't think it's a novel,' Cassie said. 'It's more like a diary.'

'Only he wrote things *before* they happened!'

'What's it say for today's date?'

No one had thought of checking on that. Molly hurriedly turned the pages to the entry. *Convocation of senior bishops at Canterbury to discuss last-minute changes in thanksgiving service.*

'*Bishops?*'

'Convocation? What's a *convocation*? Why was he writing about *bishops*?'

'I think it's a code,' Molly said. '*Bishops* means *generals*.'

'It *can't* be true!' Cassie cried. 'Look!'

She'd spotted one of *Grey Squirrel's* many grumbles, dated in February. There was a long sequence of messages telling a separate story. His first message explained that the people of 'a famous city in the Fens' were fed up with the huge concentration of artillery temporarily based there. The streets were congested, the shops were running out of food – and the dean of the cathedral had complained because heavy trucks and 25-pounders had churned up the grass on Cathedral Green and turned it into a quagmire.

You could see how each of these fragments told a bigger story. But Cassie was confused and upset. 'There *was* no congestion in Ely!' she said. 'I went past Cathedral Green every day on my way to school – the grass *wasn't* messed up! And I don't remember any artillery! We would have *seen*.'

'So would we,' Molly said. Her school was directly opposite the Green. 'Perhaps it wasn't Ely. Perhaps it was Norwich.'

'Or Peterborough,' Edward suggested.

'No!' Cassie said unhappily. 'It mentions the cannon on the green. *That's* Ely!'

What did it all mean? What was Uncle Peter up to? 'None of that ever happened!'

Baffled and confused, they gave up. Edward had brought from home the dust-wrapper of one of his favourites, *Herbert Strang's Adventure Book for Boys*. It fitted Uncle Peter's book perfectly. In its disguise it was put back on the table with the others. 'Just in case,' Edward said.

Molly, wanting to distract Cassie and change the subject, said to her, 'Did you *really* always tell the truth, you and your uncle?' she said.

Cassie wanted them to understand how seriously she and Uncle Peter had been about this. 'We had three rules. One was that we would always keep promises. The second was that we should never have secrets from each other.'

'And the third . . . ?'

'We would never lie to each other.'

Molly and Abigail shared a sideways look. Secrets were essential in their lives, each was thinking. And if you had secrets, then a certain amount of lying was necessary to guard them.

As for Adam, he rarely told lies. This was not because he was a better person. He just couldn't be bothered. And, anyway, if he had secrets from time to time, Molly and Abigail usually knew what they were.

In her trouser pocket Cassie had an old photo, shabby and worn. She took it out to show them.

Five heads gently knocked each other as they crowded over the photograph. The likeness was exact. Everyone marvelled. 'Is this you?'

Cassie shook her head. 'It's my mother. She was the same age then as I am now.'

'It *could* be you. You're exactly like her.'

'Do you miss her?'

'I was only six months old when she died.' Cassie had sometimes wondered if somewhere deep inside there lay a tiny baby-sized sorrow, a forgotten grief wrapped up in swaddling clothes and put away. But there was no trace of it – all she had was this photo, which she'd put in her pocket when she went to Uncle Peter's funeral.

On the back someone had written in pencil *Elizabeth Margaret Seymour*. 'Was that her name?' Molly asked.

Cassie nodded, unsuspecting.

'But your mother should have been called Elizabeth Margaret *Dinsdale*.'

Cassie felt herself flush all over. 'You mean,' she said in a small voice, 'that this is *not* my mother?'

Abigail took up the case. 'She's obviously your mother. You're as alike as two peas in a pod. But if Uncle Peter is your uncle, they should have the same surname.'

Then there was a disorderly discussion about other relationships – re-marriage, step-children, and all manner of different possibilities.

And a sorrowful voice from Cassie's private shadows seemed to ask softly: *Who am I?*

Much later, when it was almost dark and the others had

gone, Edward came back to the brake van with biscuits and milk for supper. Cassie had lit a candle.

She's been crying, he thought. Edward had an instinct for sadness.

'I'm sorry it took so long,' he said. (*Perhaps if I'd been quicker she might not have cried.*) 'There were things I had to do for my gran.'

She gave him one of her grave sidelong looks, which he was beginning to understand. They ate their suppers sitting side by side on the bed.

'Do you really think that man was watching for me?'

He nodded, reluctantly.

'It's something to do with Uncle Peter's book, isn't it?'

'It must be.'

'Do you miss your mother?'

'No,' he said. How could you miss someone you can't remember? 'But I do wish sometimes I could be like everyone else.'

'Oh, *yes*!' Cassie said passionately. In a rush of fellow-feeling, she abruptly stretched herself out on the bed, and wriggled along so that her head lay on Edward's lap.

He held his breath in disbelief.

'Do you like me?'

Her voice seemed to Edward to come from far off, in a strange half-lit wilderness of moon and snow. He waited for what seemed an age, and then he heard his voice replying, 'Yes.'

After a while she closed her eyes and Edward studied her mouth – barely inches away. There was a minute upward curve at each end, like the tiny beginnings of a smile. But he already knew that they were no more than the set of her features. You couldn't trust them; they were always there whether she was smiling or not. If you wanted to be certain you had to watch her eyes. They sometimes had a stern look in them, wary, challenging, looking askance. But they could become affectionate and kindly without seeming to change at all. Her mouth would widen and her face would become radiant. Then you knew.

He watched the rise and fall of her chest, and the just visible pulsing of the blood at her throat. Had she fallen asleep? *Am I going to have to sit here all night, without moving?* he thought.

Hilda Confronts the Boffins

Precisely at one minute to nine Hilda Pritt strode towards the HQ building, noting with interest that a dark staff car with an attendant chauffeur stood outside the entrance.

She'd thought a lot about what she should wear. Not her ATA uniform, she told herself, and decided in the end on a pair of German military boots that she'd found behind the pilot's seat of a crippled Messerschmitt, and a woolly top and dungarees, with a tam o'shanter on her head.

In Group Captain Rayburn's office she found not the two people she was expecting, but five. With the man in the pinstriped suit were three others, all in uniform, two Army and one RAF. They wore the red flashes that indicated they were senior staff, from headquarters.

It was a familiar situation, she thought, as old as time – a solitary woman confronting a line of men in authority. Hilda was equal to it.

The senior officer took his cane from under his arm and tapped the end of it on the desk. 'Sit down,' he said. He was tall, with a slight stoop, and his grey hair was sleeked back. There was an elegant and silvery look about him, which commanded great respect. 'I knew your father, in the Great War.'

Hilda ignored the order to sit down. 'Everyone knew my father in the Great War,' she said, '– when it suits them to say so.'

The senior army officer twinkled at her benignly. 'Is it true that you fly Halifaxes?' he said cheerfully. 'Amazing! A slim girl like you managing thirty tonnes of aircraft!'

'There's nothing amazing about it,' Hilda said icily. 'I *fly* the bally thing. I don't have to *carry* it!'

She turned to address Mr Pinstripe. 'You lied to me.'

'*Hilda!*' The Group Captain was red-faced and embarrassed – by Hilda's manner, by the way she was dressed, and because he had no idea what was going on.

The senior officer spoke. 'What did you mean,' he said silkily, 'when you said you would *blow this thing sky high*?'

'If I don't get the full story I shall inform the police. And the newspapers.'

There was a pause while the five men took this in. 'Hilda,' said Group Captain Rayburn almost in a whisper, 'you could get yourself into very serious trouble. Have you forgotten that we are all subject to the Official Secrets Act?'

But Hilda was ready for that one. 'But, Teddy darling,' she said sweetly, 'this is *not* an official secret. It's a very *un*official one. It would be my duty as a citizen to report such a mystery.'

'Now listen, young lady . . .' This came from Mr Pinstripe.

'No! *You* listen!' Hilda said. 'You sent me out to find the whereabouts of a missing schoolgirl without telling me the whole story. You lied about her uncle. *You said he was dead and buried!'*

Again, she had the sense that Teddy Rayburn had no idea what was going on. But the other four waited in silence, watching her closely.

'Now,' she said, 'Mr Peter Dinsdale might for all I know be dead. He probably is – but his body was certainly *not* in the coffin they buried at his funeral.'

'What *was* in it then?' one of them said, very softly.

'Twelve-stone of builders' sand,' Hilda said quietly. 'Ordered from London, by phone. So that the coffin-bearers wouldn't realise the coffin had no body in it.'

'Group Captain,' the senior officer said quietly, 'I think you should ask that pretty young clerk in the next room to make us some tea.'

Seated now, all of them, they added sugar, stirred their tea, fiddled with their saucers, waited for someone to resolve this difficult situation. The silver-haired one had taken Group Captain Rayburn aside and consulted him in a low voice – about me, Hilda supposed. He'll want to know if I'm reliable. And Teddy will say what a splendid chap I am, and so on and so on.

'Miss Pritt,' the air commodore said importantly.

'The whole of mainland Europe is in enemy hands. It's been like that since the Nazis drove us out in 1940, at Dunkirk.'

'Everyone over the age of seven knows that,' Hilda murmured.

'And everyone knows that this War cannot be won unless we get a toehold somewhere on the coast of the mainland. A *second front*, an *invasion*.'

'It's common knowledge,' Hilda said carefully, 'that the allied troops will attempt an invasion this summer. People discuss it openly.'

'But they don't,' the air commodore said quietly, 'discuss *when* and *where* the invasion will take place.' He turned to one of his army colleagues. 'Donald,' he said.

Donald took over the explanation. He was an erect and confident man, the sort who would succeed in everything he did.

'The invasion will certainly fail – and thousands of our troops will be killed – if the Nazis find out where we intend to land our armies. At the moment, all Hitler's troops – panzer divisions, artillery, anti-aircraft, supporting air power, and *millions* of men – are spread out from Norway in the north all the way to Italy in the south. We want to keep it that way. If he finds out where we plan to land, he will concentrate his forces in that place. If that happens, we won't stand a chance. Our second front will be annihilated in a blood bath – and this War might never end.'

She'd known all that, of course, but in just a few words he had made her care about it afresh.

'Now, what I am about to tell you *is* an official secret. *Very* official, and *very* secret. Lives depend on it. Is that clear? Good. I'll try to keep this brief. Our entire military capability is spread across three invading armies, and Hitler knows all about them. What he does *not* know is that two of them are *fictitious*. One is in Scotland, the other is here, in East Anglia and Kent.'

Hilda did not attempt to hide her surprise. It seemed too massive a deception to stand the faintest chance of success. 'How?' she said.

'We tried dummies. Inflatable tanks like balloons, whole airfields full of bombers made of plywood, that kind of thing. But they were on a very small scale. Our main strategy is to feed the enemy *mis*information.'

'Misinformation?' Hilda said, intrigued. 'How?'

'There are two main ways. There are spies, agents that Hitler thinks are working for *him*. But in fact they're working for *us*. I don't know much about them and I wouldn't tell you if I did. But take my word for it – a vast amount of *mis*information gets passed through them.'

Hilda sensed that the others were anxiously wondering just how much he was going to reveal. Rayburn, she could see, was fascinated and impressed.

'The second thing we do is to generate radio messages about troop movements *that don't exist*, vast convoys assembling, great fleets of American and Canadian planes arriving at East Anglian airbases. Military movements all over the south-east.'

He spoke softly, almost inaudibly. It was not a whisper, it was more like a distant rustling voice you might hear coming from three rooms away.

'This is done on an enormous scale. And it's all transmitted in codes that we know the enemy can decipher. Messages like *Locking pins for eight hundred 25-pounders all faulty. Send replacements.* Or *Request maps locating road bridges south-east of Calais.* Most of them are tiny details, but altogether they have created a fiction on a massive scale.'

'Does Hitler believe all this?'

'So far it seems that he does. He expects us to attempt an invasion near Calais. And that's the work that Peter Dinsdale did for us. He thought up the messages, and made sure they all fitted together like a story. He even included muddles and mistakes so that the whole thing didn't look too neat. He wasn't the only fellow involved of course. But he was the most important. *Brilliant* chappie!'

Outside, the engines of a Lancaster bomber roared briefly near the perimeter, and then spluttered into silence.

'He passed the messages to us and we sent them off from places all over the region. And that's not all. He arranged for stories to be published in local newspapers – all made up, and each one a small part of the overall picture. Let me tell you, this man was a genius. It must be like writing a war novel – only with real lives depending on it.'

'Did he hold all this stuff in his head?' Hilda asked.

'No – and that's one of our problems. He kept a book apparently. And it's disappeared! Our people have looked everywhere. If that book falls into the hands of the enemy – well, you can work it out for yourself.'

'What do you think has happened to him?'

'He vanished. Just over a week ago, at about 3.30 in the afternoon. We'd made provision for such a contingency, of course. His housekeeper also worked for us. She did what she'd been instructed to do: she'd been given a number and she contacted us straightaway.'

Hilda went straight to the main point. 'Killed? Or kidnapped?' she said.

'We don't know. *But we had to shut down the story.* That accounts for the fake funeral.'

'And the girl?'

'The housekeeper handed in her notice straightaway. She was instructed to do that – to give us a reason for taking the girl into our care.'

'Care?' Hilda doubted that these men knew what kind of care a shocked and frightened schoolgirl might need.

She saw their embarrassed looks. There had been bad planning.

'The girl jumped the gun. We hadn't foreseen that.

Ran out in the middle of the funeral service, before we could take charge of her. Had some kind of fit, apparently. She has to be found. *And* the book.'

The silver-haired air commodore took up the story. 'Dinsdale might already be dead. On the other hand he might be alive and in enemy hands. Now, he's very good at resisting interrogation – he's tough. He narrowly escaped death in Berlin in 1939. But if they've got the girl as a hostage . . .'

'And she hasn't been seen since?'

'We know she cycled to Ely. We told you – she has a favourite teacher there, where she goes to school.'

'I wish you'd told me this before,' Hilda said. She felt suddenly depressed, and hopelessly ill-equipped to help in this situation. It was unlike her to be dispirited.

'There's something else. Yesterday she phoned one of our safe houses in London. From a call box in Great Deeping.'

'How did she know which number to call?'

'We're not sure.'

'What did she say?'

'Nothing. She asked for Uncle Peter – then she took fright and rang off.'

'What time?' Hilda asked.

'Around ten pm.'

Of course, Hilda thought. She waited until after dark.

A concentrated silence fell on them as they absorbed the implications of all this. Group Captain Rayburn fidgeted, but no one else moved a muscle.

'Why do you want me?' Hilda asked. Her desire to embarrass these self-important men had evaporated. She just felt depressed.

'Because the local children will trust you. Best to keep the police out of this – security matter. We have others out there looking for Dinsdale and his book, but they work best on their own.'

Then he added, very slowly, with emphasis, 'It might be better if you concentrated your efforts on talking to local kids as we asked you, instead of following your own line.'

But Hilda wasn't having that. 'If you'd had the sense to tell me the whole story I wouldn't have wasted an entire day chasing up the mystery of the builders' sand!'

At the door she turned. '*And*,' she commanded, 'I want to know which phone box the girl used!'

Cassie, left alone in the railway van while Edward went to the shops, heard footsteps outside, shuffling slowly nearer. She stiffened, felt the hairs on the back of her neck stand on end. The man in the sinister spectacles? she wondered. Or would it be the other one?

But better to know than not. The sliding door at the end of the van was open because it was a warm sunny morning. So Cassie moved quietly to it and peered out.

There was an old woman. She was tiny and frail, moving first her walking stick, then one foot, then the other, then the walking stick again, as if every step had to be strategically worked out before it could be put into operation. When she reached the van she slowly lifted her stick and rapped on the woodwork.

Cassie's initial fear had subsided. And when there was a second imperious knocking on the woodwork, she simply stepped out onto the platform and said, 'Hello!'

Old Mrs Barrett carefully folded her knuckly hands over the top of her stick. She studied Cassie carefully, and there was no clue in her face to indicate what she thought of her. Her eyes look straight at you, like Edward's, Cassie thought. But faded and pale.

She's seeing a boy, Cassie reminded herself. 'Would you like to come in?' she asked doubtfully. She couldn't think of anything else to say.

'I can't climb those steps,' Mrs Barrett barked. 'And if I could I wouldn't be able to get down again afterwards. I don't want to die in a railway van!' *Weak body, firm words*, Cassie thought.

So she jumped down to the ground, and as she stood there she felt tall and long-legged, a lofty giant beside this small shrivelled person.

'Is he looking after you properly?'

Perhaps she might have bluffed and pretended she didn't know who *he* was. But it would have been pointless and unkind. So, since Mrs Barrett was clearly a woman of few words, Cassie's reply was equally direct.

'Yes. He's very good to me.'

It was a strange moment. Nothing more was said, and yet Cassie felt as if the two of them had shared a long conversation. The old lady began a slow turn – a sequence of shuffling movements of her feet – and it was clear that she was about to head for home.

'Would you like me to walk with you?'

'That would be helpful. Thank you.'

So, stooping a little beside this tiny person, Cassie walked with her, and Mrs Barrett, holding her stick in one hand, put the other on Cassie's young arm. Their progress was slow – through the wood to the bottom of the garden, and up the garden to the back door of the house.

Please don't let her fall! Cassie prayed inwardly.

At the back door, they stood still for a moment as Mrs Barrett braced herself for the two steps that had to be climbed there. Then, summoning her almost-exhausted energy, she heaved herself up into the kitchen. Cassie followed, knowing that she had to see this fragile old lady safely to a chair.

In the living room Mrs Barrett managed a small spurt of energy to get herself to her armchair. The stick was placed carefully against the wall, and she put her hands onto the arms of the chair and lowered herself slowly down with a deep, thankful sigh.

A single bed, neatly tidied, stood against one wall. And a wooden commode.

'Now,' Mrs Barrett said, 'pass me my Bible. It's on the table.'

As they'd walked through the trees, Cassie had had an absurd idea. Now she took the bull by the horns. 'Mrs Barrett, may I have a bath?'

'Of course! A girl has to keep herself clean.'

Cassie stared at her.

'Why didn't he bring you here, to the house?' Mrs Barrett said. 'You don't have to sleep in a railway van.'

But Cassie stayed loyal to Edward. 'I like it there,' she said.

'He has his own way of doing things,' the old lady said. 'The bathroom's upstairs. You'll find everything you need.'

24
Pepper and Curls

The five met in town after dinner, Cassie newly clean and refreshed. When they reached Uncle Peter's house they walked slowly up and down the street, and around the cricket pitch at the back. They saw no one suspicious. The policeman had gone.

So they took up the positions they had agreed, and Cassie and Abigail went in through the gate at the bottom of the back garden.

Abigail had drawn the short matchstick to go with Cassie. 'You scared?' she whispered.

'I absolutely am!' Cassie said cheerfully. *But it's my house*, she kept telling herself. *It's where I live. I won't be stopped from going in!*

She found the spare key where she knew it would be, inside a split in the bark of the tree that bore the weight of her tree house. Abigail shivered as Cassie unlocked the back door.

Inside, the house was as silent as the grave, emptier than all other emptinesses.

'The clock has stopped!' Cassie whispers. They stand

for a moment, listening to the clock not ticking. The house holds its breath and all the objects in it are waiting and watchful. Time has died out, and come to a close.

'I'm going to start with the kitchen.'

'Why are you whispering?' Abigail asks, whispering herself.

The boy-Cassie looms a little in the shadows of the back hall. 'Don't know,' she says, still whispering.

'What do you want me to do?' Abigail asks.

Cassie is vague. As she goes into the kitchen she says, 'Have a look round.'

First Abigail goes into the dining room. From there she can see the back garden – and the top of Molly's head beyond the fence. No danger there. Molly is where she should be, keeping watch. Then she goes back into the hall and peers out of a front window. Edward is standing faithfully by a telegraph pole a few houses down the road. Adam is sitting on a wall, drawing in his sketch pad. All is well.

Abigail sets off to climb the stairs, ascending into a different kind of emptiness, brighter and sunnier but just as silent. Halfway up, where there is a turn in the staircase, she stops and listens to the silence. Above her, level with her head, there is a huge bookcase on the landing, and four doors leading into four rooms. Each will have its own emptiness, bereft by death.

This is silly! she tells herself – and climbs the last steps to the landing.

One of the doors has a label glued on it with *Cassie's*

Room – Private written in childish handwriting. The door is ajar, and Abigail slowly pushes it open, and steps inside.

And then . . .

From the threshold where she stands Abigail looks slowly round Cassie's room – where nothing stirs in the bright still sunlight.

But where there is sunlight there are shadows. On an upright chair in the darkest corner of the room sits a man, motionless, silent, with a gun in his hand, and his hand in his lap.

For what seems like a whole minute but is probably barely more than a single second, she stares at him. Then he leaps to his feet and lunges grotesquely towards her across the front of a dressing table. Abigail backs out of the bedroom. She has a speed-of-light understanding that if she tries to run downstairs he will be able to shoot at her down the stairwell. So she ducks in the opposite direction, through a door facing the top of the stairs.

She has turned to the right but he first looks left, downstairs. And in that instant when he is looking the wrong way Abigail throws herself at him sideways, using her favourite football shoulder tackle. She has done this a hundred times in games with the others. It is a ruthless and well-practised manoeuvre.

She is a strong girl, almost a young woman, and she catches him off balance. He staggers helplessly, and plunges sideways down. Abigail grabs the banisters to stop herself from falling with him. She stares as he crashes down, and his gun slips from his grasp and flies upwards in an elegant lob and eventually clatters onto the floor of the hall.

Would Molly have been as brave if she'd been there? Yes, undoubtedly. But she wouldn't have been as quick. She would have wanted to work out the consequences – and she would have considered the fact that people pushed downstairs are sometimes killed.

Molly would have pondered all this, and lost her chance.

And Adam? He would probably have shouldered the man so hard that he sent him crashing to his death.

This man, though, is not dead. He has clearly been taught how to fall. He somehow rolls himself into a protective ball and stops halfway down, where the staircase turns a corner.

Now Abigail is trapped. As the man unfurls himself halfway down the stairs, she makes a dash for it, racing down and leaping over him. But he has recovered himself quickly and he reaches out one hand and grabs her by the ankle, bringing her up so sharply that she falls headlong and only just manages to raise both hands to save her face from smashing against the wall.

But Cassie is there. In her hand is a tubular cardboard container. She dashes from the kitchen to the bottom of the stairs, pulling off the lid. Then she empties the contents all over the man's head and face.

There is an instant explosion of gasps and coughing.

He cries out and swears, waving his hands about and releasing Abigail's foot.

'*The back door!*'

They are outside in an instant. As Cassie relocks the door with trembling fingers, they can hear the banging and bumping inside, as if the man is throwing himself about. But Cassie, listening for a moment, feels no pity, and Abigail grabs her hand and pulls her down the garden.

In less than a couple of minutes all five of them are racing across the sports field to the churchyard where they'd left their bikes.

'If you find yourself in trouble and you happen to be in a kitchen,' Uncle Peter had once said to Cassie, 'you should try *pepper*!'

Mr Tittipat's personal telephone rang.

'Yes?'

'Two kids broke in, sir. A boy and a girl.'

Mr Tittipat's voice was cool, barely interested. 'When?'

'Ten minutes ago.'

'And of course they got away.'

''Fraid so, sir.'

'Have you caught a cold, Wilson?'

'No, sir. The girl was her, sir.'

'Describe her.'

'Quite tall. About fourteen. Long hair.'

'Colour?'

'Fair, sir.'

Mr Tittipat took a deep and bitter breath and replaced the receiver on its hook.

Hilda Pritt – on her way through the town – saw five young people cycling towards her at great speed. *I say!* she thought to herself. *Isn't that Adam What's-his-name? It jolly well is!*

And who were the other four kids with him? *That's Molly Barnes*, Hilda thought. *Gosh, she's grown! When I was that age I was as flat as a tea tray!*

The five young cyclists were in a great hurry. None of them noticed Hilda, who lowered her foot to the ground and hop-stepped her bike to a standstill, looking back over her shoulder to see the children turn into a side street that led towards the common.

I must, she thought, *pay them a visit and question them about Cassie Covington. They seemed jolly excited about something.*

Thoughtfully she remounted and resumed her journey.

In the safety of Edward's railway van the five heroes talked about what had happened again and again until every last drop of dramatic juice had been squeezed from the story.

Abigail felt a retrospective terror that she hadn't felt

at the time. 'If it hadn't been for Cassie . . .' she said. She couldn't stop saying it, and she couldn't stop shaking.

The first to come down to earth was Cassie, who said in a grandmotherly voice, 'Let that be a lesson to you. Always have some *pepper* handy.'

The others waited.

'Put it on everything,' Cassie said. 'On mashed potatoes, on fried eggs, on strawberries. *Especially* on strawberries.'

'And intruders!' Adam said.

'Abso-bloomin-lutely!' Cassie said.

But Abigail was muted, still troubled. 'What's wrong?' Molly asked her.

Abigail shrugged, in a way that meant there was more she could say if she chose. '*Tell* us!' Molly insisted.

Abigail chose her words carefully. 'This isn't a game,' she said. She hadn't ever thought that Cassie had been *lying*. Not exactly. But she'd never quite believed her either. But now – with the skin on her ankle still red (almost *burned*) where that man's hand had grabbed it – there could be no more doubting. 'There really *is* something strange going on,' she said. She stared unhappily at her ankle, wishing she could wash off that man's touch.

Cassie, who understood what Abigail meant, said, 'I wonder if it was the same man I found in my bedroom, that afternoon. What did he look like?'

But Abigail had never had a chance to memorise his face.

'Did you find anything?' she asked Cassie. That, after all, had been the reason for going to the house in the first place.

'Nothing definite,' Cassie said. 'But . . .'

'*But?*' They all stared at her, impatiently waiting.

'There *was* one thing. We keep a calendar hanging in the kitchen. And Uncle Peter *always* wrote on it the date and time of every phone call.'

Where was this leading? they wondered.

'On the day he died, he'd written in a phone call from Dame Lily at my school.'

What's so important about that? their faces said.

'But when Dame Lily had a message for him, she always gave it to me to take home from school – if it was a school day. It happened several times.'

'Perhaps she couldn't find you at school?'

Cassie shook her head, working it out. 'She phoned him at 3.35 that afternoon. Five minutes before that she'd been taking my class for English. Our last lesson was with her.'

'So why did she have to phone him?' Adam said.

'Because,' Molly suggested, 'the message was *urgent* – and it couldn't wait until Cassie got home.'

Cassie nodded slowly. 'I think she knew something – and rang to warn him.'

'And when you got home from school, an hour later . . . ?'

Cassie nodded slowly. 'He was dead. Or vanished.'

Or dead and *vanished*, Molly thought.

Outside, in the trees, someone was listening.

That afternoon there was a walker in the fields and footpaths around Deeping. He surveyed the landscape and the sky with apparent pleasure, and in time he approached the distant end of Barrett's Wood.

When he came to the abandoned railway track he turned along it and went into the trees, warily now, less briskly. About a quarter of a mile into the wood he stopped, looking puzzled, as if something he had expected to find there had been unaccountably taken away.

He stood still for a while, thoughtfully stroking his chin. Then he spotted some distinctive rust marks on the rails – eight of them – and came to the quick conclusion that the railway guard's van he'd been expecting to see there had been towed away. And the coal wagon that had been with it.

He followed the railway tracks deeper into the wood, more cautiously now because he knew he was coming closer to the house where the owner lived, old Mrs Barrett. And soon, in the near distance, he spotted the missing brake van and its companion coal truck.

And he heard voices. *Young* voices.

He crept as close as he dared. The conversation was a chaotic scramble of voices, each seeking to be the loudest. The intruder circled the brake van, stepping carefully through the trees and paying attention to those voices. There were, he felt sure, at least two girls in that van. Perhaps three. He took note of two metal hasps, one on the sliding door and one on the door frame. He was good at spotting things, always had been.

Then he stopped.

At his feet, among the generations of dead twigs and blackening leaves, were some clusters of snipped-off hair. Long, dark-brown hair, glossy in the afternoon sunshine.

That evening, Hilda Pritt cycled back to Fen Common and stopped by the phone box. She could see in the distance – barely half a mile away – a wood. A *large* wood! It was beyond the cottages that flanked the common, and she could see that a narrow lane led into it.

There would be lots of hiding places in a wood, Hilda thought.

She walked her bike slowly along the lane, passing a solitary house and crossing a disused railway line.

In such a perfect early-summer evening, with low sunlight slanting through the fresh green of the trees, it was hard to believe that all along the south-west coast, thousands of troops were preparing for the biggest invasion in world history, the attack that was intended to be the turning point of the War.

If that girl is hiding here, Hilda thought, *she's unlikely to come out until after dark*.

The floor of the wood was covered with bluebells. They were lovely beyond words. Hilda had never seen bluebells horizontally, only from high on horseback. Quietly she walked into the silence of the trees, feeling sentimental about England and bluebells.

She reached a place where the railway line stopped at a large crater filled with thick and flourishing cow parsley. A dead pond, she thought vaguely. Then, as she picked her way round the edge to rejoin the line on the other side, she stopped and stood motionless, holding her breath.

She could hear singing. Not *just* singing – Hilda thought it was the sweetest voice she had ever heard! The song was 'Home Sweet Home'. Hilda – who could barely endure her own home for more than a few hours – had heard the song a hundred times, sung drunkenly in pubs, and in that horrid way they sang songs on the Third Programme. But this was different, lovely beyond all loveliness! *This* brought a lump into her throat.

She stepped forward and discovered that the sound was coming from an old railway brake van that stood among the trees. Laying down her bike, Hilda approached cautiously, and as she drew nearer she could hear that someone was humming softly in unison.

The singing stopped abruptly. They'd heard her.

After the slightest of pauses – during which Hilda was thinking fast – the door at the end of the brake van was opened and two boys came out onto the platform.

'Hello!' Hilda called out gaily. 'I didn't mean to interrupt you. *Sorry!* Gosh, what a wizard place! I *say*, is this yours?' She indicated the railway van.

They said nothing, but the taller boy pointed at Edward.

'Which of you is the singer?'

Edward pointed at himself. Then, feeling it was his duty as owner, he asked Hilda if she was lost, and did she need any help.

'It was the bluebells,' Hilda said, lying shamelessly. 'I flew over this wood the other day and – do you know? – I could see the blue through the trees! It can't be true, I thought. So I came to see.'

'*Flew?*'

'Yes. I was bringing in a Halifax.'

They were hooked at once. It always worked with kids. 'Were you piloting it?' one of them asked.

'Of course.'

She could see they were impressed, and in only a few more moments she had been invited to join them inside. She peered around like a good-natured older sister inspecting a children's den. In reality she was hoping to spot an unnoticed feminine giveaway – a skirt perhaps, or some stockings.

But there was nothing. She was invited to take a biscuit from a rusty tin, and given a glass of squash from a jug. And in return she told them about being an ATA pilot – about take-off and landing, about being shot at by mistaken British anti-aircraft, about the time she'd been chased by a blinking Meschersmitt and could only escape by climbing – against all the rules! – into thick cloud.

'Why is it against the rules?' Edward asked. 'Don't you have instruments for navigating?'

'We're not trained to use them,' Hilda said. 'And we're not allowed to make wireless contact.'

'How do you know where you're going then? Or where to land?'

'The same way you ride a bike – by *looking*!' Hilda said. 'Which is why clouds are jolly bad news.'

They were fascinated, both of them, bewitched by her stories of real flying. Even the shy tall one who hardly spoke at all.

'I say! Do you know Molly Barnes?'

The smaller one said yes, they did.

'And Adam? And Abigail?' Hilda said eagerly. 'I stayed at the guest house once, some years ago. We had a bit of an adventure . . .'

But she had no reason for staying. So she thanked them for the biscuit and drink, and turned to leave. As she stepped down to the ground, she turned back. 'Did you know that girl everyone's talking about? The one who's scarpered?'

They shook their heads gravely.

'But you have heard about her?'

'Yes,' Edward said. 'But she went to a different school.'

The boys went back inside, and Hilda walked off along the railway track.

However, she was suspicious and she had no intention of leaving yet. She found a place where the trees were thickest and there was a fallen branch to sit on. She felt a growing sense of triumph.

She didn't have to wait long. The two boys came out onto the platform at the back of the brake van, jumped down to the ground, and walked into the trees.

Then they stood side by side, looking down and concentrating, with their backs to Hilda and their hands in front of them. When they'd done they trooped back to the brake van.

'I *can't* pee like a boy!' Cassie had said when Edward explained his idea. They had watched Hilda through the narrow window in the side of the van, outraged by her duplicity, untroubled by their own.

'You can *pretend* to do it like a boy,' Edward said patiently. 'At that distance and with our backs to her, she won't be able to see.'

'You're a genius!' Cassie said when they were back inside. 'A hero *and* a genius!' *I've saved her from capture,* Edward thought proudly. *A second time!*

'Dash it!' Hilda muttered. She'd been absolutely certain that the small one had been a girl in disguise. A girl's voice, surely! And such a lovely face!

A brand-new Lancaster roared low overhead as she walked back to the road and she watched it longingly. How much easier flying was than this bally detective work!

❧

Meanwhile, the sharp-eyed countryside walker was making a phone call.

Each speaker knew who the other was and no words

were wasted. 'That dog that ran away – I think I know where it is.'

'The bitch?'

'That's the one.'

'Jolly good! Tell me all about it.' The cheerful voice concealed tension and urgency.

'I was looking for that old toy train.'

'But we're no longer interested in that. None of the children have played with it for years!'

'I know, but it's been moved and I wanted to see if I could find where it had been put.'

'Moved, you say? Did you find it?'

The telephone operator, if she'd been listening in, would surely have grown bored by now.

'Yes. Some other kids have been playing with it.'

'Go on.'

'I think they've got our missing pup – and they've cut some of its hair off. I found a stack of it nearby, under the trees.'

'Are you sure? Is the hair the right colour?'

'Yes.'

There was a pause while the speaker at the other end took this in. Then, thoughtfully, 'We can't let them take possession of our pup.'

'What do you want me to do about it?' He knew the general answer already – but not the precise degree of it.

'Get hold of it – if the damned thing will let itself be brought home.'

The countryside walker waited, needing an even more specific instruction.

'Of course, it may have to be destroyed. Terribly sad, I know. But that's what happens to mad dogs. They can be *dangerous*. And this one . . .'

'When?'

'Tomorrow. There are things we have to get ready. Oh! and that other thing we've been looking for, keep an eye out for that. The pup might have run away with it – *and it's even more important than she is.*'

The connection was cut off. The country walker held the receiver in his hand a few moments more, thoughtfully stroking his chin.

Hilda arrived at St Dorothea's in the lunch hour.

She remembered staying at her own school during the half-term holidays, when she used to help the housekeeper to sort the bed linen, and the girls had had free run of the tennis courts and the swimming pool.

A groundsman with a very odd beard straightened up from his gardening. On seeing Hilda's uniform he instantly clicked his heels together and saluted. *Ridiculous*, Hilda thought.

As she waited in the entrance hall, Hilda studied the school's honours board and chose a name at random. *Doris Heathcote*. She had about fifty degrees after her name. *Some kind of super-swot*, Hilda thought.

She was shown into the school library where Dame Lily was seated at a table. The teacher leaned across to shake hands with Hilda and knocked over a pile of exercise books.

Hilda helped her to pick them up, and then said, 'I do apologise for coming to see you on a bank holiday, but I don't have many days free.

'– It's my niece, you see. Looking for a place in a good boarding school.

'– Father's away. Mother's gone orff with a Yank.

'– I'm not her guardian, of course. Just trying to help. It's down to me to find the right kind of school.'

Dame Lily smiled. This was someone she knew how to handle. 'Why St Dorothea's?' she asked.

'One of my pals came here. Doris Heathcote. Awfully nice gel! She heartily recommends St Dorothea's.'

'Doris!' Dame Lily said thoughtfully. 'I was her form mistress. Clever girl! Teachers never forget, you know. Close friends?'

'Not really,' Hilda said sadly. 'I see her from time to time. She went into academia and I took up flying.'

'And you're looking for a boarding place for your niece?'

A girl of about ten had come into the library and sidled close to Dame Lily. Her eyes were filled with tears, and it was obvious that she was in search of sympathy.

'Not now, Felicity,' Dame Lily murmured gently. 'I have a visitor. I'll be free in a few minutes.'

'But, miss, it's Julius!' the girl wailed.

'What's the matter with Julius?'

'He's broken his leg!' – and as the enormity of it hit home the poor girl began weeping openly and noisily.

'Is Julius your brother?' Dame Lily asked.

'No! He's my *pony*!'

'Oh, I say! That *is* serious.' Dame Lily put her arm around Felicity and hugged her sideways. 'Now, Felicity dearest, as soon as I've finished talking to my visitor, you and I will have a chat. I promise.'

163

There weren't any teachers like that at my school, Hilda thought.

Felicity disentangled herself and walked disconsolately out of the library, leaving Hilda to run through a long list of hurriedly prepared questions about uniforms, laundry, and fees. Finally, when she thought she'd played the role of the caring aunt to the point of exhaustion, she changed the subject. 'One of your gels is in a spot of bother, I've heard,' she said innocently.

'She's not in any *school* bother,' Dame Lily said. Then she added, 'I suppose you are referring to Cassie Covington?'

'I think that was the name,' Hilda said vaguely. 'Hasn't she disappeared or something?'

'Well, you see, her poor uncle has died. He was her guardian. We believe she's run away because she's unhappy.'

'Did you know him?' Hilda asked.

Dame Lily stared hard at Hilda to indicate that she was stepping where she had no business. 'Yes, I knew him well,' she said. 'It's awfully sad.'

'I would have thought,' Hilda said, 'that the child might have come here if she was unhappy.'

Dame Lily closed down the conversation. She rose to her feet, saying, 'I will ask one of the lower sixth girls to show you round the school.'

She walked across to a beautiful dark-haired girl wearing a prefect's badge and standing by the fiction shelves. 'Prudence, dear, I wonder would you show our visitor . . . Oh, I say, Prue! Are you sure you're *ready* for *Lady Chatterley's Lover*? It is the French edition, you know, with nothing left out.'

Prudence looked witheringly at Dame Lily. 'Well, *you* put it in the library!' she said.

'Because it's Great Literature,' Dame Lily murmured. 'And I knew the author . . .'

Prudence replaced the book on its shelf, and braced herself to take Hilda on a tour of the school.

What a bore! Hilda thought.

'You used the wrong tense,' Prudence said as they walked into the big assembly hall.

'What?' What *was* the girl talking about?

'When you said Doris Heathcote *recommends* this school.'

'Why?'

'She died years ago! She was killed by all that studying, I suppose. There was a big fuss, and we had a memorial service.'

St Dorothea's was exactly what a girl's boarding school should be like when most of the pupils were on half-term holiday. Hilda was reassured by the sense of familiarity. But if she'd been a trained detective, she might have wondered why Dame Lily hadn't challenged her about the Doris Heathcote lie.

Hilda wasn't a detective – but neither was she stupid. That question settled itself in her mind, like a seed preparing to germinate.

～

Molly and Cassie sat by the river that afternoon with their feet in the water, a girl and a boy side by side. With them was Molly's little brother, naked, wading cautiously in the water. *He's like an extension of his sister*, Cassie thought. *Quiet, watchful.*

Molly had something on her mind. 'On the day your uncle died . . .' she began.

She saw Cassie take a deep breath, bracing herself.

'. . . did you see him when you got home from school? I mean, did you see his body?

'No. There were two men.'

She stopped. The memories came back in fragments. 'Our housekeeper was there. She said he'd been taken away.'

Another fragment came; Miss Jardine's white face.

Molly understood it all – Cassie paralysed by confusion and distress, unable to question what she was told. *That's enough for now*, she thought, and she changed the subject.

But Cassie also had a tricky question to raise. 'That photo of my mum,' she said. 'With her name on the back . . .'

'Elizabeth Margaret Seymour,' Molly said. (*She remembered!* Cassie thought in surprise.) 'I've been thinking about that. There can only be three reasons.'

Cassie lifted her feet out of the water, drew her

trousered knees up to her chin, and gazed across the big wide river.

'Your grandmother might have married twice. People do. If your uncle was born in one marriage and your mother in the other, they would have had different surnames and she would be his half-sister.'

But that was not possible. Uncle Peter used to tell her stories about his childhood. *Lots* of stories. There had been no mention of his mother having married twice. And there'd been no sister in those stories either.

'Well then, your grandfather might have had a love affair with someone. And she had an illegitimate baby.'

It was the forbidden subject, never discussed except in low voices. But Cassie – who had known the facts of sex since she was seven – took it calmly. 'I don't think so,' she said. 'According to Uncle Peter, his mum and dad were childhood sweethearts and happily married for years.'

'But would he have told you? Perhaps it was hushed up.'

Cassie shook her head. Uncle Peter had never hushed up anything to do with sex. 'He told me everything,' she said.

'Then there's only one other possibility,' Molly said. 'He wasn't your uncle.'

Cassie dipped her feet back into the water, shivering briefly at the chill. *There goes my only remaining certainty,* she thought. *Now what?*

Molly opened a paper bag with three sausage rolls.

She handed one to little William, standing in the water up to his middle, and another to Cassie. They ate companionably.

There was a young couple on the river. A soldier – in uniform except for his cap and boots and socks – was rowing strongly upstream. His girlfriend's feet were bare too, and she pressed them against his as he rowed. As they passed, the soldier winked at the boy and girl on the riverbank.

'He thinks we're . . .' Molly said.

'Weird!' said Cassie.

'Abso-bloomin-lutely!' they said in unison.

Three sudden swifts, swooping low and squealing, scooped the river and were gone. And Molly said out of the blue, 'Edward likes you. A lot.'

Moments passed. Cassie was at a loss, with no idea how to reply.

In the river young William's feet slipped in the mud and he unexpectedly found the water up to his chin. He scrambled hurriedly onto the bank, bare and goose-pimply, and went to Molly, who wrapped him in her woolly cardigan and cuddled him.

'He's very young,' Cassie said, meaning Edward, not William.

Big things are often decided by little things. There's an old poem that speaks of an entire kingdom lost – all for the want of a horseshoe nail. In Cassie's case it was the other way round. Her life was *saved*, not lost.

And all for the want of a chamber pot in Edward's railway van.

Soon after midnight when Cassie awoke, she knew she would have to go. It was a nuisance, but the night was warm, and she slipped on her sandals and went out as she was, in pyjamas.

Everywhere was still, enchanted by moonlight. As she was about to set off back, she saw a shadow moving in the trees close to the guard's van. She ducked low, and watched.

It was a man, wearing some kind of mask. Something like a woollen balaclava, she thought. It gave his head a distorted look, swollen, with a big chin. This was bad enough, but he also had a gun, a hand gun of some sort, aimed ahead of him as he moved.

He is looking for me, she thought. *Here we go again, Cassie Covington!*

When he reached the railway van he quietly circled

it. Then he stood motionless, facing the door that Cassie had left open. She was motionless too, watching him through the trees.

Never attack an armed opponent, Uncle Peter had told her, *unless you have a secret weapon of your own.*

Well, she hadn't. So she waited and watched. After several minutes, the intruder stepped up onto the platform at the end of the guard's van, and Cassie saw that in his other hand there was a large torch. He switched it on and stepped inside.

Her thinking was quick. It would take him only a few seconds to find there was no one in the van.

That's how long I've got to get away, she told herself. She set off at once, treading as soundlessly as she could on the twig-littered floor of the wood, in a wide circling movement. When she reached Edward's back garden, she would be able to move more easily on the soft and silent grass.

Should she hide? There were possible places among the trees and undergrowth. But no, it would be better to seek Edward's help. So she raced silently up the garden towards the house to wake him up.

But how? If she knocked on the door his grandmother would wake up too. Or she might be so frightened by loud noises in the night that she died on the spot.

Her mind sorted the possibilities with speed and urgency. And at the back of all those thoughts there was another: *I am scared, but not terrified. I can cope with this.*

She knew that Edward's bedroom was at the front of the house because when she'd had her bath she'd taken a brief look. So she hurried round to the front of the house and threw a handful of earth at his window.

She was stooping for another handful when she became aware of a movement at the side of the house. Had she heard it? Seen it? Or just *sensed* it? She was sure there had been a slight disturbance in the shadows.

Someone was moving cautiously along the path that led from the back garden to the front.

Cassie gave up on Edward, raced into the lane, and fled.

Then she set off at a run across the town to Paradise Barn – an enchanted journey through midnight streets, with the houses on each side looming solidly between deep caverns of darkness. Bedroom windows were open because of the warmth of the night and behind them a whole population was sleeping.

– except for one old man who was awake and restless, seated by his window. Night after night, he watched the empty street in which nothing ever happened. Then he saw with perfect clarity a boy in pyjamas, jogging past in the middle of the street. Like a solitary fish swimming upstream, he thought.

Cassie reached the other side of town and set off along the field path that led to the barn, which she could see, hunched in its own massive silhouette. She knew that the horrible man with the thick glasses might have the barn under surveillance, but she no longer cared.

Not once, she thought, *have I given way to panic.* But now she wanted company.

Edward *had* been woken – but very slowly. As soon as he was fully conscious he hurried to his window and looked out.

There was no one. Cassie was already in the lane, racing away. The intruder was there, but Edward couldn't see him in the shadows by the corner. Had he been dreaming? But when he pushed up the bottom half of his window he saw fragments of earth on the sill.

The intruder heard the sound of the window being opened and saw someone looking out. After a few moments he turned and walked carefully back along the side of the house, down the back garden, into the trees, and towards the brake van.

He would wait all night, if necessary.

And Edward? He knew it could only have been Cassie, and he knew she was in trouble. It took him barely two minutes to creep downstairs, slip on a pair of sandshoes, unbolt the back door, and set off in the moonlight towards his brake van.

Edward was on a rescue mission.

Breathless from running, Cassie pressed her back against the towering wall of Paradise Barn and scanned the fields in the clear moonlight. But there was no figure moving over the moonlit fields. No one had followed her and everywhere was still.

Her breathing slowed, and she was struck by how amazing it was that she should be there, pretending to be a boy, racing through town in the middle of the night in someone else's pyjamas, probably pursued by a masked man with a gun.

She realised with a shock that a part of her enjoyed this, and was excited by it. *Hmm!* she thought. *It must run in the family. Uncle Peter was a man of danger, and perhaps she too* . . . But then she remembered Molly's doubts about her uncle's uncleness and she put him out of her thoughts. For the time being.

She slipped through the half-open door of the barn, and walked cautiously across the pitch-dark space to the stairs against the far wall. She put one foot on the bottom step and shouted.

'Molly! Abigail!'

There had been so much silence that her calls seemed outrageous in the quietness. They startled her as much as they startled the three sleepers.

Upstairs, Cassie took in the scene – Molly in blue pyjamas kneeling up on the bed and rubbing her eyes; Abigail in a white nightdress lighting a candle and cupping the flame with her hand; Adam, bare-chested, half in and half out of his sleeping bag on a mattress on the floor.

Cassie's account of what had happened was urgent and to the point, and their sleepiness was banished at once. 'Let's go and see!' one of them said eagerly. There was no hesitation, no planning. The four of them would be invincible. Obviously.

'Wait!' Abigail said. 'I've got to get dressed!'

'No one will see you,' Molly said.

But it wasn't decency that Abigail was worried about. 'I can't *run* in a nightie!' she declared. Cassie – startled, slightly shocked – waited while Adam searched for his pyjama top, Molly put her shoes on, and Abigail changed into shorts and shirt.

But downstairs, she took charge. At the door of the barn she flung her arms wide and held back the other three. 'Wait!' she whispered. Carefully she studied the fields for signs of a pursuer. Then, 'Let's go!'

In no time at all they were in the town, jogging steadily and quietly through the darkened streets, one dressed for the seaside, the other three in pyjamas. Not one of them gave any thought to the fact that they were going in search of a man with a gun.

The elderly watcher who couldn't sleep was still at his window. There were more of them this time, moving downstream together, a shoal of four. The old man watched intently, spellbound by night magic.

Edward, single-minded in his purpose, moved quietly through the trees towards the brake van, silent in the tree-dappled moonlight.

First he walked all round the outside, then he stepped

cautiously onto the platform. The sliding door was open, and he moved into the darkness of the interior.

But there was enough light for him to see at once that Cassie wasn't there. Her blankets had been thrown aside. He racked his brains, working out different possibilities. She might have gone outside for a pee – but why then would she try to wake him up? She might have been captured – but how then did she manage to throw earth at his window?

The brake van moved imperceptibly. Only its owner would notice such a slight shift, and only its owner understood what it meant. Edward knew he was trapped. He turned to face whatever was coming.

At the open door the moonlight was obscured by the bulk of an intruder, and a torchlight was shone into Edward's eyes.

'Light the lamp!'

It was a low growl of a voice, accustomed to giving orders. Edward felt for the box of matches, spilt some of them as he fumbled a single one into his grip, and set its shaky flame with trembling hand to the round wick of the paraffin lamp.

As they faced each other in the yellow lamplight, Edward took in the lumpy masked head and the shining eyes flicking their glance from side to side with an angry and ferocious greed.

And the gun.

'Where is she?' the intruder demanded in a fierce gravel voice.

Once, several years ago, Edward had done something very brave. But he'd been so young that no one knew whether he understood the danger he'd been in. However, let there be no doubt about this time. He knew exactly the situation he was in, and he braced himself to face it.

When he heard those words *Where is she?* he felt a surge of triumph. They meant that Cassie was somewhere else. He didn't know where – but nor did the man with the gun!

'I said: *where is she?*'

'Who?' Edward said, wide-eyed with puzzlement.

'You know who! The girl you've had living here.'

'My mate's been sleeping here. Tony.'

A sarcastic sneer. '*Tony!*'

'Yes, Tony Cassell.'

The intruder gave up on that line of enquiry and cast his eyes around the van. Edward knew at once that he was hoping to see Uncle Peter's book, which stood alongside several others, disguised as *Herbert Strang's Adventure Book for Boys*. And he knew he must distract him.

He picked up a leather purse and threw it on the table. 'Is this what you're looking for?' he said.

The contents of the purse poured out onto the table-top. Thirty pieces of silver. Thirty German reichsmarks.

Edward fully understood the danger he'd placed himself in. The intruder was breathing heavily, as if troubled. Or angry. 'You,' he said slowly, 'are going to regret this. I know exactly what to do with uncooperative boys!'

The words were chilling. But his actions were less sure. Despite what he said, he did *not* know what to do. Finding a boy – a boy who knew that the guard's van had once been a safe house for spies – had not been part of the plan. He needed further orders.

Edward was surprised when the man took from his pocket a large padlock. He'd come prepared. 'I'll be back in fifteen minutes,' he said. 'And you'd better spend that time thinking about the worst things that might be done to you! And even then you'll be *wrong*! What will happen –' he spoke the words very slowly '– Will. Be. *Worse*.'

Edward watched him go out and slide the door shut. There was the metallic sound of the padlock being slotted through the hasps and then snapped shut.

Edward made himself wait for several minutes, until he was sure the man had gone. Then he shifted the table to one side and moved a chair. The intruder didn't know – and hadn't noticed – that brake vans always have a door at both ends.

It was stiff, this other door, because it was hardly ever used. But Edward forced it open, grabbed Uncle Peter's book, and slipped out into the night.

And the intruder? What about him?

He'd hurried along the lane towards the telephone

box on Fen Common, rehearsing in his head what he would say. *The bitch isn't there. But there's a pup. A young male. I've locked it up for safety. What do you want me to do with it?* Once he had his orders he would be pitiless.

But there was a problem. Everyone knew that bored telephone operators at the exchange sometimes listened to conversations as they went through. Especially in the middle of the night. The dog code might not be enough.

No, he thought. *I must deal with this myself.*

Keyed up for action, he hurried back to Barrett's Wood, where he found his pup had escaped. Probably hiding in the trees, he thought. Or gone home. He made a half-hearted search for a while, but then he gave up and left.

He was angry and mortified. *Very* angry. *But a man of action*, he told himself, *always knows when a mission should be aborted.*

❦

Cassie, Molly, Abigail and Adam, hurrying through the streets, met Edward on his way to them.

The insomniac old man, seated at his bedroom window, saw the four children in the street below him met by a fifth – another boy – who'd come running to meet them. He was briefly hugged by one of the group. *Strange! Boys didn't hug each other in my day*, he thought.

He watched eagerly as they whispered among themselves, and then set off back. Upstream this time.

When the five friends were safe in the barn at last, they gave way to triumph and jubilation. They had a midnight feast of sorts, although it was long after midnight, and not much of a feast.

Then – as dawn lightened the sky – Edward remembered that he was on the wrong side of town. So, still in his pyjamas – and accompanied by Adam in case of public embarrassment – he went home to get dressed. And to see to his grandmother's needs.

Where's Cassie going to stay now? he wondered unhappily.

Later, back in the barn – washed, dressed, and eating beans on toast for breakfast – that was what they talked about: *Where could Cassie stay?*

'Here!' Abigail suggested. 'You could stay in our barn.'

But after one more night, the others would be sleeping at home again. 'I daren't stay here at night by myself,' Cassie said. *Not in this huge empty place, alone in the dark*, she thought.

Edward tried his luck. 'You could stay in my house. There are two spare bedrooms. We would have to do all the work because my gran's too ill now. She doesn't do the cooking any more. And she can't climb the stairs.'

And to Edward's secret joy they worked out how it could be done. It began to be possible.

But other questions crowded in. What would Cassie do all day? What about school? How long could she stay disguised? They all knew in their hearts that her troubles were too big for them to deal with.

'We should talk to Hilda Pritt,' Adam said. 'She would help us.'

Hilda was in Adam's mind because the previous day they had found a note pinned to the door of the cabin:

> Molly. Can you all come home tomorrow at about ten thirty? Hilda Pritt called today hoping to talk to you about something. I'm sorry to interrupt the last day of your holiday, but she said it was important.
>   Love, Mum.

'We've got to talk to her anyway,' Adam said. 'So why don't we tell her everything?'

'We know Hilda Pritt,' Molly explained to Cassie.

'But she *spied* on us the other day in the wood! I don't trust her,' Cassie said.

'Hilda's all right,' Adam said firmly. He had always admired Hilda, ever since he'd known about her flying.

'What else can we *do*?' Molly said.

'Edward's *told* you what we can do!' Cassie said. 'I can hide in his house.'

Adam looked her straight in the face. 'How long for?' he said.

Cassie's good temper deserted her. 'I *hate* you, Adam Swales!' she snapped. 'It was you who brought these two in! If you'd kept your mouth shut we wouldn't be in this mess!'

Molly leapt at once to Adam's defence. 'That's not fair! You would have been caught if it hadn't been for us.'

'When?' Cassie demanded.

Abigail chipped in. 'In your house the other day.'

'*And* last night,' Molly added. She remembered Cassie's fear.

So far, they'd been carefully polite to each other, guardedly edging their way into a new friendship. Even overdoing it a little. But that was all set aside. This was raw and naked fury.

'You three didn't do anything last night – that was Edward.' (Edward was excluded from her anger.)

'Well, who did you come to when you couldn't wake Edward? *Us!*'

'I'd have been better off on my own!'

'Well, go and *be* on your own then!'

'And who was it who managed your disguise? Us!'

Edward looked unhappily from one speaker to the other as they argued. He knew nothing about rows. He had no brothers or sisters, and his best friend at school was Adam, who never quarrelled with anybody.

'She'll have me put in some kind of prison for kids.'

181

'No, she won't! We'll make her promise not to.'

'Hilda's not like that!'

'Yes, she is! She'll be *just like you!*'

'Cassie Covington, that's a horrible thing to say!' Abigail retorted. 'We haven't broken any promises.'

'Well, you want to now. You will if you tell that woman about me!'

They went on for ages, verbally slanging and banging each other. With Uncle Peter, such outbursts had usually ended with him ruefully flapping his hands at the point where he was about to give in. But these three did *not* give in. So Cassie, beaten and frustrated, stood up and said, 'I'm *going*!'

'*Where* are you going? You haven't got anywhere to go to!'

But she'd left and was stamping down the staircase, leaving the others looking at one another, shame-faced and rueful but still angry. 'What else could we *do*?' Abigail said.

Edward knew what to do. He raced out and down to the floor of the barn. He got to the big barn door before Cassie reached it and turned to face her.

Her eyes were wet and blazing. 'Don't go,' he said. '*Please!*'

But Cassie couldn't speak. She shook her head fiercely, took him by the shoulders and pushed him to one side. 'Then I'm coming with you,' he said. (Because, if the person you're rescuing runs away, it means you've let them down. The least he could do was go away with her.)

And they were gone, almost, when Molly, hurrying down the steps from the cabin, shouted across the barn. 'Cassie! Wait!'

And that made Cassie hesitate. Edward stopped too – and in that instant the others appeared at the top of the steps. All five came together again, just inside the big barn door.

Their difficulty remained precisely what it had been before: Adam still thought they should confide in Hilda; Abigail was still angry; Molly remained upset because Cassie had said she hated Adam; and Cassie felt betrayed. So nothing had changed – and yet everything had changed.

Quarrels do that sometimes. They just run out of energy. Suddenly they all wanted to be friends again.

'You look a bit of a mess,' Adam said.

Cassie, rubbing her face with the back of her hand, wished she could think of a clever retort. Where was Uncle Peter's remembered voice when it was needed? But Uncle Peter was silenced and Cassie was on her own in an unfamiliar country. 'What's the point of staying here,' she said. 'if you're going to tell that woman about me?'

Then Edward said, 'I've got an idea.'

29
Hilda Makes a Bargain

There was no time for Edward to explain his idea because someone was crossing the fields towards the barn. Hilda Pritt – in uniform – was about a hundred yards away.

'She's coming to talk to us,' Molly said. 'About you – almost certainly.'

Cassie was aghast. 'I don't want her to see me! I won't be able to fool her twice!'

'Get back upstairs and under the bed,' Adam said.

'Why? Will she be coming up there?'

'Of course she will. She's coming to talk to us.'

Cassie was desperate. 'But what will you say?'

'Edward's got an idea,' Molly said. None of them knew what Edward's idea was. Would it amount to anything?

They all stared at him. 'Well,' he said . . . But there was no time to hear Edward's plan. Hilda was almost upon them.

'Get upstairs and under the bed!' Adam said. '*Now!*'

'But she'll hear me breathing.'

Abigail's patience was exhausted. 'Then *don't* breathe!'

Cassie looked at Edward for a fraction of a second. It meant: *I am putting my fate into your hands*, and he understood. Then she raced across the barn and up the stairs. As she disappeared into the room at the top, Hilda Pritt stepped into the barn below.

'I *say*! It's jolly good to see you all again!

'– You've all grown since we last met! Grown-ups always say that, I know. Must be jolly irritating!

'– When was it? 1940? Gosh! It seems an age ago!

'– And I know you too! You're the boy in the railway van. Where's your tall friend? Do you know, I thought at first that you were a girl! Embarrassing confession, I know. Can you imagine anything so ridiculous? A *girl*! It was because of your singing.

'– Up these steps? What a lovely little room! You *are* lucky! I *say*!

'– Where shall I sit? Here? Are you two comfy on that bed?

'– Jolly good! I know what you're thinking, Molly. I was supposed to be meeting your mother this morning. And I will, later. But I thought I'd rather speak to you first.

'– What? Oh, well, I thought there might be things you don't want her to know about.

'– Well! Down to business. Thing *is*, I've been given a job. And I need to pick your brains.'

But Hilda was not feeling as confident as she sounded. As she contemplated the four young people in front of her, she found them more daunting than the high-ranking officers she'd faced at the airfield – two well grown girls; a young boy; and Adam Swales (she remembered him well).

She came quickly to the point. 'It's about this missing schoolgirl. You've heard about her, of course?'

They nodded. She was impressed by their silence, their seriousness. 'I'm involved in the search for her. And I need you to tell me if there's anything you know about her whereabouts. Anything you've heard from your friends.'

Hilda had not expected much from this interview but she sensed at once that they were waiting, watchful. 'Well?'

The three older ones were looking at the younger boy – Edward, was it? – as if he was the one who had the information. Hilda began to feel hopeful. Just a little.

'We know where she is,' Edward said. 'She's in hiding.'

Ah! Tricky, Hilda thought. 'Where?'

'We can't tell you. She doesn't want anyone to know. She doesn't want to be found.'

First things first, thought Hilda. 'Is she all right?'

'Yes, she is. She just doesn't want to be found.'

Hilda drew in a big breath. 'This is not a game,' she said quietly. 'You must understand – this girl . . .'

'Cassie,' Edward said.

'Yes, Cassie. She could be in danger. I think she *is* in danger.'

'We know that,' Abigail said. 'A man with a gun came looking for her! Of *course* she's in danger.'

Hilda looked alarmed. 'Did he find her?'

'No, she got away,' Edward said.

These children were in deep, Hilda realised. And so was she.

'And there's that horrible man at the guest house,' Molly put in. 'The one with the thick glasses.'

'Oh, *him!*' Hilda said breezily. 'He's one of our lot.'

'Is he looking for Cassie too?'

'No,' Hilda said cautiously. 'Well, not exactly. A more general line of enquiry.' She took a deep determined breath. 'You have got to tell me where she is.'

What should Edward do? What was best for Cassie? Would she forgive him if he broke his promise, if he gave her away?

Hilda, beginning to suspect that she was not going to be told, tried another tack. 'Why does she want to stay in hiding? She'd be safer with the authorities.'

Edward answered, methodically explaining. 'There are two reasons. The first is that she will be taken away and put into some place like a prison. You'll say it's a school, or a special home, but she'll be a prisoner there whatever you call it.'

Hilda sighed. There was no answer to that. 'And the other reason?' she asked.

'She thinks – *we* think – that her uncle might not be dead. She wants to stay free until she can find him.' Edward lost his confidence at that point. It was suddenly clear to him that this was a stupid idea, a pretend game that small children might play. He waited for Hilda to scoff.

Hilda didn't scoff. 'But he was buried,' she said quietly.

∾

'If,' Hilda said slowly, emphasizing the *if*, '– if Cassie's uncle is alive, it's possible that he is being held prisoner somewhere.'

Then she added, 'Until the invasion.'

There was a pause, then a question. 'Then they'd let him go?'

'He would be of no value to them *after* the invasion has happened. He's only useful to them if they can get information from him in advance.'

Abigail was the first to understand. 'But they wouldn't dare let him free,' she said quietly, 'because he would know who they were.'

'So Cassie's uncle . . . ?'

'They would have no more use for him,' Hilda said. Her words were like crisp round pebbles dropped one by one into a cold glass bowl.

Not in her wildest imaginings had Hilda anticipated a conversation like this. Confronted by this earnest boy, she came close to letting her personal nature overrule her professional self. She was seriously tempted to break the Official Secrets Act and tell them everything she knew. 'Look here!' she said. 'You have to tell me where she is. For her own safety.'

At this point, Molly intervened. 'But what good would it do?' she said. 'She wouldn't go with you, even if we told you where she was.'

Molly had touched a sore point. This had worried Hilda. At the back of her mind she'd always wondered how she was going to take charge of this runaway schoolgirl if she refused to come quietly. She could hardly take her to the airfield at gunpoint. Or whip out some handcuffs and frog-march her to the nearest bus stop. No, if Cassie Covington chose not to cooperate, what could Hilda do?

'I have an idea,' Edward said quietly.

A silence descended on them. A waiting silence.

And into the silence Edward said, 'There's a book. It belonged to Cassie's uncle. It's full of secret information to do with the invasion.'

Peter Dinsdale's book! Hilda flushed with excitement. Surely they hadn't . . . ? They couldn't have!

'Wait!' she said. She went to the door of the room, and stood for a few moments at the top of the steps. When she was satisfied that no one was there she returned and shut the door. 'Just checking,' she said. 'I assume there isn't anyone hiding under the bed.' It was a joke.

'To people in the government that book is probably more important than Cassie is,' Edward said.

Oh, wise young man! Hilda thought. But she would never admit such a cruel thing to them. 'Do you know where this book is?'

Edward nodded. And he almost said: *We have it. And we will give it to you if you make us a promise.* But what he actually said was, 'I have it. And I'll give it to you if you make me a promise. A bargain.'

This was Edward's idea. This was what everything depended on. And he knew that Cassie – under the bed – would be paying passionate attention.

'A bargain? *What* bargain?'

'If you promise to leave us alone to look after Cassie, we will give you the book.'

As Hilda took in the implications of this, Adam chipped in. 'Your bosses would be awfully pleased with you if you could give them the book.' (*Adam never says awfully*, Molly thought.)

Yes, Hilda thought to herself. *They would. But could she make such a deal? Dare she do it? Suppose this girl got hurt? Or worse?*

'Why is this book so important?' Abigail asked. 'It's all scraps and scribbles!'

Again, the Official Secrets Act came close to being fractured. 'There's going to be an invasion, everyone knows that,' Hilda said cautiously. '*Soon* – and it'll be a jolly big show. Everything depends on it. Hitler thinks we'll invade across the narrowest bit of the English Channel. He's prepared for that.'

'But we're going to invade somewhere else,' Adam said. 'And take them by surprise.'

Hilda stared at him. She could not say yes or no to that. 'It is vital,' she said carefully, 'that the German high command continues to believe the invasion will be around Calais. Information has been fed to them for months – *mis*information. It all had to hang together and to sound right. That's what Peter Dinsdale did – he masterminded it all. And it is all in that book. That's how he held it together, by writing it down.'

Under the bed Cassie adjusted her view of Uncle Peter.

'If it were to fall into the hands of the enemy . . .' The War had toughened Hilda. She was not as breezy as she'd been in 1940. She was war-weary like almost everyone, tired of danger and anxiety. Her brother was at that very moment commanding his unit down in Weymouth. Waiting, with hundreds of thousands of others. There was a seriousness in Hilda's voice which they'd not heard before.

'If this book falls into the hands of the enemy, it will take them barely ten minutes to work out what it's about. And if the information reaches the German high command . . . Well, thousands and thousands of our troops will be massacred.'

Edward stopped her. 'Well, we have it,' he said.

'Can I see it?'

Edward shook his head. 'Not until you promise.' His voice switched unexpectedly into a croak. It irritated him because he had no control over it.

How different this boy was from those shifty men from the War Department, Hilda thought. How reluctant they had been to reveal the full truth! But this boy was direct and straightforward, and already she knew that she would accept his terms. She would have to.

'All right. But I'm going to give you a phone number and you must promise to phone me if there's trouble. That's *my* side of the bargain. There's a password, too. It's *Sleeping Beauty*. You can use the phone on the common near where your wood is.'

'We can't use that,' Abigail said. 'It's under surveillance.'

Hilda stared, realising – not for the first time – that she should never underestimate these kids.

'But do you promise?' Edward said.

'Yes. I've said.'

'You have to say the words.'

'All right. I promise not to reveal that you know where Cassie Covington is hiding. In return you have to give me Peter Dinsdale's book, and promise to contact me every day.'

Then Adam intervened. He had thought of a possible trickery here. 'What's to stop you from following us, or spying on us, so that we lead you to where Cassie is?'

'Well, I won't. I just won't.' It was a feeble undertaking, but what else could she say? 'I promise I won't.'

Adam (*Serious?* Molly wondered. *Or just messing about?*) said, 'Tell you what! If you also promise not to spy on us, I will draw you. A proper picture.'

The conversation changed gear immediately. Hilda was startled to find that she felt a shiver up and down her spine, as if she was suddenly naked.

Perhaps he knew this. 'Either in your uniform or in civvies,' he added.

But Hilda was already having second thoughts about that bargain. 'How will you manage? Has she got her ration books?'

'No, but I have my grandmother's – and she hardly eats anything.'

'Money?'

'Well, I have some . . .'

'Take this,' Hilda said. She took five pound notes from her purse and handed them to Edward. It was an enormous sum. 'Now the book, please.'

Edward handed over Uncle Peter's book. It had been on the table all the time, lying among schoolbooks and sketchbooks, and wearing the jacket of *Herbert Strang's Adventure Book for Boys*. Hilda took it, removed the dust-wrapper, and opened it.

Was she going to read it all? They longed to be rid of her, and to let Cassie out from under the bed. As for Hilda – scanning the pages – she knew at once the importance of the prize she held in her hands.

'What's she like, this Cassie?' she asked.

'She's lovely,' Edward said.

This boy needs to grow a protective skin, Hilda thought. Instinctively, she looked at Adam. Did he too think the missing girl was lovely?

'I like her feet,' Adam said, leaving Hilda feeling slightly out of her depth.

Molly and Abigail, waiting outside the headmistress's office, sat side by side on the Bad Bench, opposite a large mirror. Their reflections stared nervously back at them, framed.

The holiday had ended, the mattress and blankets in the barn had been taken home, and school had started again – and they'd been summoned out of their history class to see the headmistress.

Molly studied her reflection. Eyes watching watching eyes. She was conscious of the body inside her blouse, and the balance of her bones, womanly and confident. But her reflection showed a nervous schoolgirl in uniform.

Miss Sweetly (*Sugarlump*, the girls called her) was a new kind of modern headmistress. That day she wore a light pair of tasteful shoes; her skirt was of an expensive cut and material; she wore a dark red, high-necked blouse; and she had on long earrings that emphasised the elegant line of her neck.

'Come in, my dears,' she said. 'Please sit. Of course, you know what I wish to discuss with you.'

'No,' they said. (This was not strictly true. They both

suspected – with a sinking of the heart – that it had something to do with *Daisy Daring*.)

'Comfortable? Good! Now, my dears, I could hardly believe my eyes when one of the prefects brought me this.'

They'd been right. She took *Daisy Daring* from a drawer, and laid it on the desk. 'A first-former was looking at it,' she added. 'It had been passed round among them.'

Miss Sweetly smiled at them, woman to woman. She was good-humoured and disarming – lightly laying before a pair of wilful youngsters the folly of their conduct.

She bashed the book lightly with the back of her hand. '*This*,' she said, 'is very silly. Very childish. Now, my dears, you do see that?'

They'd hardly spoken so far. Abigail murmured that it was just a story.

'It's too silly for words,' Miss Sweetly replied.

Molly couldn't resist it. 'It's hardly *got* any words!' she said. 'It's a *picture* story.'

'It's based on Jane in the *Daily Mirror*,' Abigail explained. 'And that's not childish. This month it's all about *careless talk costs lives*.'

'And your point is?' Miss Sweetly probably didn't read the *Daily Mirror*.

'It's patriotic!'

'Well, clearly, we have a difference of opinion.' Miss Sweetly smiled.

(From another world, they heard the girls of the fourth

form trooping in from the tennis courts. '*Straight sets!*' somebody shouted triumphantly. 'Would you *believe* it?')

'I might not have minded if that's all it was. A piece of rubbish, no more. But there's *this*.'

She turned the pages and found a picture of Daisy stepping into a bath. 'Do you think this is . . .' she hesitated – '. . . suitable? Appropriate?'

'Why isn't it?' Molly asked, knowing perfectly well.

Miss Sweetly smiled again. 'Molly,' she murmured, 'this young woman is wearing no clothes.'

This was too much for Molly. 'She's having a bath!'

'Indeed she is. But did she have to?'

'But that's the joke – Daisy reveals everything to the reader but nothing to the Nazis. The strip's joke wouldn't work if she didn't.'

Do I really believe that? Molly wondered briefly. She wasn't sure. She'd only just thought of it.

Miss Sweetly winced as if she'd just had a whiff of a disgusting smell. 'Oh, really!'

She directed her next question at Abigail. 'Abigail, do you too fail to see how bad this is?'

'She's only bare!' Abigail retorted.

'That might not matter,' Miss Sweetly said, 'if one were on a remote Greek island. On a warm beach perhaps. But in a girls' school in England, it really won't do.'

(The bell rang for change of lessons. Doors slammed and several hundred pairs of feet clomped on the wooden floors and staircases.)

'Which of you drew this?' she asked softly.

No reply. 'Molly?'

Molly sighed deeply but still made no reply.

'Abigail?'

Abigail was more direct. 'Neither of us drew it,' she said firmly.

'Then who?'

Everybody thought Molly was a quiet and law-abiding girl – and so she was for about three hundred and sixty-four days of the year. But she was capable of rare and startling acts of determined rebellion, and Abigail sensed that a rebellion was about to burst out. Under Miss Sweetly's table, she put her foot on Molly's and pressed down hard.

Miss Sweetly tried a different approach. 'Secrets are a kind of lying, don't you think?' she remarked quietly.

No, they're not! Molly thought. Abigail – who could hardly believe they had been tipped into this trouble when they had intended no harm at all – said, 'It's not our secret. So we can't tell.'

And that, she thought, should have been enough. But Miss Sweetly persisted. 'Who,' she said quietly, 'is this Daisy based on – bare and having her bath?'

They didn't know where to look, wished they were somewhere else, and said nothing. (Daisy's hair was short like Abigail's, but dark like Molly's. Who, they'd asked Adam, *is* she? No one, he'd said. She's a blank. That's the point!)

'Very well! I'm afraid I have to take a severe line on

197

this matter. I'm going to ask you to leave the school this afternoon.'

'We're being *expelled*?' Abigail's words shot out, unthought. It was too awful to grasp.

'No. You're being *suspended* – until you decide to tell me who drew these pictures.'

'But it's so unfair! It's just because Daisy's naked!' Abigail sounded almost triumphant, as if Miss Sweetly had been caught out.

'The whole thing – the whole book – is childish, badly drawn rubbish! And you brought it here to be passed around in my school!'

'That's unfair!' Molly declared.

Miss Sweetly seemed genuinely to want the girls to understand her difficulty. 'This school is a business. I know that you and some of your friends are on scholarships. But most parents pay fees – *and they don't expect their daughters to be exposed to indecent pictures.*'

'When have we got to go?'

'Oh, straightaway.'

They stared in disbelief. It was too awful.

'You can, of course, avoid this if you choose to tell me – now – who drew these pictures.'

Silence.

'Very well. I will have to write to your mothers,' she said cheerfully. 'But I shan't do so until tomorrow afternoon. If you choose to come to school tomorrow and tell me the full truth, then we need say no more about it. You have until tomorrow afternoon to think it over.'

Hilda also had a difficult interview that day.

This time, there were only two of the senior staff, Group Captain Rayburn and Air Commodore Willett. The older man was curt. 'You have it?'

'This is it,' Hilda said.

He frowned when he saw the cover. But he took the book, sat down at Captain Rayburn's desk, and leafed his way through the pages.

Hilda had thought there might be some signs of excitement, or triumph, or at least relief that Uncle Peter's book was in safe hands. But Air Commodore Willett took his time inspecting the book and showed no emotion at all.

'And the girl?'

Hilda had been dreading this question. 'I can't tell you where the girl is,' she said.

'If you don't know where the girl is, how did you get hold of the book?'

Hilda didn't answer this question directly. How could she? If she told them about the promise she'd made, they would think she'd taken leave of her senses.

But Edward had been right. The authorities were far more interested in the book than they were in the girl. No more was said to Hilda about Cassie.

Then Hilda put a question to them. 'The search for Peter Dinsdale – has there been any progress?'

'We're fairly certain now that he did not go voluntarily.'

'How do you know?'

'If he'd told them what they wanted to know, there would have been major enemy troop movements on the mainland of Europe. There have been none.'

'So he was –' she hesitated, '– *taken*.'

'Almost certainly. But we know nothing else – and, if he's still alive, time is running out for him. When the invasion takes place, they will have no further use for him. Anything he can tell them will be out of date.'

'So they'll let him go?' Hilda asked. But she didn't believe it.

The older man stared at her, stony-faced. 'I doubt it,' he said.

Then Captain Rayburn put his oar in. 'Well,' he said, 'he's already had his funeral.' And Hilda thought that was one of the stupidest things she'd ever heard anyone say.

Edward was in a state of rapture at the thought of Cassie moving into his house. She'll be able to sleep in a proper bed again, he thought, and use a proper bathroom. He anticipated her pleasures.

On their first morning, he spent half an hour with his grandmother, and then he and Cassie – still in pyjamas – had their breakfasts in the kitchen, exchanging brief companionable remarks. Afterwards he left to catch his train to school, and she went upstairs to get dressed and washed.

Later, Cassie knocked quietly on Mrs Barrett's living-room door, and went in.

The old lady, in a thick dressing gown, with a rug over her knees and a bible on her lap, looked slowly up. 'So!' she said. 'You've moved in.'

'Yes.' Cassie knew she ought to have said *thank you for having me*, but she sensed that this old person was not interested in politeness. She used words only for important matters.

The old lady nodded slowly. Then she opened her bible and peered down at it. Cassie knew the conversation had come to an end.

The days passed, lonely, dreamy and unhurried. Cassie went cycling each day, exploring the countryside. If she found a café, she bought herself a midday meal. Provided it was cheap, you could do that without using coupons from your ration book.

The evenings were full of homework and gossip in Paradise Barn. Adam made drawings, almost non-stop. And Cassie quietly fretted about Uncle Peter. And her own uncertain situation.

Friday was very warm and Cassie went by train to Hunstanton. Molly and Abigail – barred from school – might have gone with her, but they were not in the mood for seaside. They planned to go to Ely on the school bus, like exiles haunting the frontier they were forbidden to cross.

Cassie found the small seaside town spread wide and open to a tranquil sky. Breathing in the sea smell and listening to the unceasing cry of gulls, she felt as if she were all air and spirit, free of solid substance. *Is it all right for me to feel so happy?* she thought.

But she couldn't stop herself. Her fears and uncertainties fell away and the whole lovely world seemed to be expanding and free, welcoming and generous, calling to her, full of promise.

The local people were going about their business in a subdued way. *They're waiting*, she thought. *Like everyone in the country, they're waiting for the big news*. And she felt she wanted to reassure them, to fill her lungs with the bright summer air and shout to them that everything would be all right.

She walked on the wide and limitless sand, with the tide rippling rapidly in. There was only one other walker, an old man with a beard and a small dog which lolloped up to her and wagged its rear end cheerfully. The dog's owner found a breaker to sit on and remained motionless there, hunched like a Toby jug, with both hands grasping the top of his walking stick.

I'm standing on the edge of the limitless sea, Cassie thought poetically. And then she thought, *I'm standing on the edge of the limitless universe!*

And then she thought, *Oh, for heaven's sake, talk sense, Cassie Covington!*

In a reckless mood she walked into the waves, still wearing her shoes and socks, not bothering to roll up the bottoms of her boys' trousers. Did she care? Absolutely not! What got wet would later get dry. With the water up to her knees she turned and walked along, splashing and kicking, with her arms swinging and her head lifted.

The little dog barked to see such silliness, and the old man stroked his beard thoughtfully. *I ought to write a poem*, Cassie thought.

By the time she had walked back to the railway station her shoes and trousers had dried out, leaving salty stains. But the poem never got written.

On the train she fell to daydreaming about beards. Long straggly beards like the old man's, short stumpy beards, beards trimmed neat and close. She tried to imagine Edward with a beard. And Adam.

~

On Monday afternoon, Miss Sweetly, walking elegantly around in her office while reading a letter, paused by the window and looked down into the street.

Her eyes fell on a boy in school uniform who stood on the opposite side of the street looking intently across towards the main entrance of the school. She watched him as he crossed the road and approached. He disappeared from sight, below her.

Adam stood still for a moment in the entrance hall, shadowy after the brilliance of the afternoon outside. A notice directed all visitors to the secretary's office, but he ignored it and followed instead a sign that pointed to the headmistress's room upstairs. He could hear the sounds of lessons – voices muffled by thick doors, a sudden burst of classroom laughter.

He knocked on Miss Sweetly's door.

'Come in!' she said, and stared in surprise when a schoolboy – the boy she'd seen in the street – walked in and closed her door behind him. Neither of them spoke at first, and Miss Sweetly watched with interest as this unlikely visitor looked around her room, taking in its details.

'Can I help you?' she asked, with a hint of sarcasm.

Either he ignored it, or he didn't understand facetiousness. 'I'm Adam Swales,' he said. 'I drew those pictures. Those *childish badly drawn* pictures.'

'Did you indeed?' she said slowly. She was adjusting her thinking, rapidly rearranging her view of things. 'Shouldn't you be at school?'

Adam ignored that question. 'You shouldn't have punished Molly and Abigail,' he said. 'They were protecting me.'

He took a few steps towards her. He could see *Daisy Daring* lying on Miss Sweetly's desk.

'So now that you've owned up,' said the headmistress, 'you expect me to let them off.'

'Yes.'

No *please*, but no rudeness either. Just *yes*.

There was a long thoughtful pause. 'Very well,' she said at last. 'They may return to school tomorrow.' (Miss Sweetly never said *all right*. It was always *very well*.)

'You were going to write to their mums,' Adam said. He was persistent.

'The letters have not yet been sent.' They were, in fact, in her in-tray at that very moment – they had been since Thursday – waiting for her to sign them. 'But I will have a chat about this with your headmaster at the grammar school.'

Again, Adam made no reply. He cared nothing for head teachers' chats.

'And I shall, of course, confiscate this.' She indicated *Daisy Daring* where it lay on the desk.

Adam shook his head. 'No,' he said. 'You won't. It belongs to me.'

And Miss Sweetly was left to stare in surprise as this schoolboy picked up the book of drawings from her desk, turned, and walked out of her office.

Why didn't she stop him? But by the time she'd raced around her desk and across the room he would have been out of the door. And it would have been unseemly to chase him down the staircase and into the street. *All good reasons*, she thought afterwards.

32
Death Comes A-Calling

Cassie woke to find Edward standing by her bed, white-faced. Her room was filled with morning sunlight.

'It's Granny. She won't wake up.'

Cassie got out of her bed, and sat on the edge of it, waiting.

'I can't wake her up,' he said.

She followed him downstairs to the room where Mrs Barrett had been living, thinking as she went that she didn't want to do this. In fact, she wasn't sure she *could* do it. But when they reached the door she went in with him anyway. She thought she would be scared but – in all truth – there was nothing scary there. The old lady lay in her bed, with her eyes shut, as if asleep. There was no movement, no life.

Edward stood back a little, waiting for Cassie's judgement. Cassie stepped back too, and they stood there side by side, and helpless.

'Is she dead?' he whispered.

'I think so,' she said. *But,* she thought, *I'm not an expert. I didn't see Uncle Peter when he was dead. Possibly because he never was.*

'What have I got to do?'

Her heart went out to him then. He wanted to do the right thing even in this situation, which he was too young – they were *both* too young! – to deal with.

'I think you have to phone the doctor.'

He stared at her in confusion. 'But he won't be able to . . .'

'I know,' she said. 'But it's what you have to do.'

So Edward, a little shakily, went out into the shadowy hall and phoned Mrs Barrett's doctor. He remembered the number; he'd phoned him a lot recently. Cassie stood beside him as he talked into the phone. *What will happen to him now?* she wondered.

An instinct of good sense directed her. She made Edward go into the kitchen with her and bullied him into making some toast, boiling a kettle for tea. It was breakfast time anyway, but she thought he needed to keep occupied. The toast was hardly buttered when the doctor arrived.

Cassie slipped quickly upstairs and crouched on the landing where she could hear most of what was said. Doctor Yorke was kind-hearted and efficient. He knew better than anyone in Great Deeping what Edward had done for his grandmother in the last few weeks.

'She was very proud of you,' Cassie heard him say as he was about to leave. 'She said so, many times.'

Then Edward asked Cassie's own question. 'What will happen to me?' he said.

'I'm not sure,' Doctor Yorke said. 'But first someone has to phone the undertaker. His name is Mr Ross. He will arrange everything and tell you what has to be done. His number is Deeping 57. Would you like me to do it?'

Edward nibbled feebly at a slice of toast while they waited for the undertaker to arrive, and Cassie – finding herself hungrier than she had a right to be in that situation – ate a full breakfast, and more. They still felt they should be quiet, although there was no one to overhear them.

A long black car drew up in the lane outside. With a quick frightened glance at Cassie, Edward jumped to his feet and hurried to the door to greet the undertaker. Cassie, hiding upstairs again, eavesdropped.

Mr Ross, too, was gentle towards Edward. 'It's usual,' he said, 'for the body to lie at home until the funeral. But your grandmother asked me some time ago to make a different arrangement. She is to lie at the Salvation Army Hall until she's buried. They have agreed.'

Two men came in from outside with a stretcher and after a few moments they passed back through the hall, carrying it carefully – out of the door, down the steps, and out to the long black car. It was a bad moment. Cassie saw that Edward was shivering. The old lady's death had become an absence now. She was gone, really gone.

At the door, Mr Ross turned back. 'I've already phoned Mr Cheadle,' he said. 'He's your grandmother's lawyer. He'll be here soon. Will you be all right by yourself until he gets here?'

Edward – confused and wanting to be left alone – nodded vaguely and said thank you.

Cassie hurried downstairs. 'We've time to get dressed,' she said, 'before the solicitor gets here.'

But Mr Cheadle was not the next person to arrive. They heard a clamour of voices outside. The others had come to call, unaware of what had happened. But their cheerful Saturday mood was subdued at once. They had known and liked Edward's grandmother.

Poor Edward! Molly thought. And then she thought: *I hate it when things change,* forgetting how fast she was changing herself.

As Edward stood lost in his own kitchen, there was a heavy knock at the door.

The last visitors at Edward's house that morning were Mr Cheadle the solicitor, and with him a Woman from the Welfare. Cassie daren't risk being recognised by the man who was legally responsible for her, so – again – she stayed out of sight in the passage. But the others stood with Edward while Mr Cheadle explained. He too was very kind. 'I'm not going to read you the will,' he said, 'because you wouldn't understand most of it.'

He underestimates young Edward, Molly thought.

'But I can tell you what's in it. Your grandmother left a sum of money to the Salvation Army – but the rest of her money and the house – *and* Barrett's Wood – all belong to you now, young man. To be more precise, I have to look after it until you're twenty-one, and *then* it will be yours.'

But Edward didn't care what would happen when he was twenty-one. 'What will happen to me *now*?' he said in a small voice.

It was the Welfare Woman's turn to speak. 'Edward, your grandmother found a place for you,' she said carefully, watching his face. 'In case this happened.'

This was news to Edward. 'My grandmother! What sort of place?'

The Welfare Woman bit the bullet. 'An orphanage,' she said quietly.

'Where?' he said almost inaudibly.

'In the Midlands,' she said. 'It's an orphanage for girls really. But because of the War, they have a few boys too. It's called St Ursula's.'

'It's very well known,' Mr Cheadle said. 'The children are treated very well.'

Probably everyone expected some tears then, or a stubborn refusal. But Edward had always known that this would one day be his fate. 'But what will I do until I have to go?' he said in a croaky voice.

Is it grief that makes my voice do that? Edward wondered. *His voice is breaking*, Cassie thought.

Mr Cheadle stepped cautiously. He was reluctant to take this boy into his own house, just as he hadn't wanted to take in that tiresome Cassiopoeia Covington. But nor did he want the boy to run away. 'Is there anyone in Deeping who would take you in for a week or two, now? Just until we get it all settled?'

Edward stared as this sank in. So many loved things

211

were coming to an immediate end. 'I can stay here,' he said hopefully.

The others knew this would not be allowed.

'I'm sorry, no. We have to find someone.'

'There isn't anyone,' Edward said.

'Yes, there is!' Molly said. 'My mum will let Edward stay with us.'

Mr Cheadle brightened. 'Are you sure?' he said. 'You're Mary Barnes's daughter, aren't you?'

'Yes. She likes Edward. She'll *want* him to stay with us.' Molly had no doubts.

That was all very well, Edward thought. 'But what about Cassie?' he said later. 'What will *she* do?'

33
Dame Lily Comes to Mind, Twice

Hilda Pritt always tried to keep her promises. So she was determined that she would not search for Cassie Covington, either openly or sneakily.

But it wasn't easy. She would be deliberately *not* carrying out her special assignment.

Instead, she set out to discover as much as possible about Peter Dinsdale. So she began noseying about with anyone she met in Great Deeping. She was unembarrassed and shameless about this, entering into conversation with shopkeepers, postmen and bus conductors. If they hesitated, she disarmed them by laughingly admitting that she was *a very inquisitive person*.

She quickly learned that Cassie's Uncle Peter had been greatly liked; that he'd been eccentric and outspoken; and that he'd been besotted with Dame Lily at St Dorothea's. As for the girl, no one knew much about her. She kept herself to herself, people said.

'What about the housekeeper?' Hilda asked. Hard as nails, they told her. Did all their shopping and housework, and cleared off at the first chance.

The vicar's wife had not been helpful. She had plenty to say about Cassie Covington's character ('Wilful! And utterly spoilt!'), and even more about Peter Dinsdale. ('Hadn't the faintest idea how to bring up a young girl!') In fact, she'd talked until Hilda had been driven almost crazy with boredom.

'Now if that English teacher had married him, *she* might have made a better job of it!'

It always comes back to Dame Lily, Hilda realised – and finally, troubled and thoughtful, she went to Mr Cheadle's offices and asked to see Mr Tittipat.

He looked up from his desk. His fat frog eyes stared at her icily.

Why have I come here? Hilda thought. To cover her hesitation she sat down, uninvited, facing his desk.

'I'm Hilda Pritt,' she said.

He waited, staring at her.

'You know who I am?'

Mr Tittipat sighed and said, 'Of course.'

'And what I'm doing?'

He saw that there would be no peace until he said something to this tiresome woman. 'You found the book,' he said.

Hilda adjusted her uniform skirt over her knees.

'And those idiots in the military,' he said softly, 'haven't understood that if you knew where the book was you must also know where the girl is.'

Hilda was irritated. The military top brass *were* idiots, but they were *her* idiots and she felt loyal to them. 'They do know,' she admitted bitterly. 'But they don't care about her. Any more than you do!'

Again he studied her carefully. 'Have you any basis for that remark?'

'None at all,' Hilda admitted. (*It's just that you look like an odious and unfeeling slug.*)

'Pay attention,' Mr Tittipat said. The words that came out of his mouth were clipped and chilled, and they created an icy stillness in the room. 'I have a job to do. It is a small but not unimportant contribution to the Allied War effort. If I'd been born a German, I would be playing a similar role for the Nazis. Feelings don't come into it – any more than you would allow feelings into the work you do, flying those planes.'

Here Mr Tittipat had made a mistake. Hilda's work *flooded* her with feelings. She *loved* those planes!

'Oh,' he said quietly. 'I see I was wrong.'

Could he read minds?

'And,' he went on softly, 'I doubt if any of those senior military idiots told you what a clever little girl you've been.'

He *could* read minds!

'I think you were a *very* clever little girl.'

Was he sneering at her?

'Now we've got that out of the way,' Mr Tittipat said, 'tell me why you've come here.'

'Dame Lily,' Hilda said.

'What about Dame Lily?'

'You've interrogated her?'

He stared, saying nothing at first. And then, '*You* must not question *me*,' he said. 'It is an impertinence.'

215

'There's something not quite right about her.'

Mr Tittipat waited for her evidence.

'It's a hunch,' Hilda confessed.

'A *hunch*?'

'I don't normally believe in women's hunches,' she said. 'When they're about *men*. Or life in general. But a *woman's* hunch about another *woman* . . .'

She saw at once that she'd caught his interest. There was the briefest frowning of his brow. What Hilda could not know was that Mr Tittipat *adored* his mother. She often discussed her hunches with him – and he always listened respectfully. All his life he had listened to his mother – and learnt, and learnt, and learnt.

The rest of that day passed quickly enough for Edward. In the morning they moved his things into Mrs Barnes's guest house, and in the afternoon they went by bus to Ely to see *National Velvet* at the Rex. Everyone felt he should be kept busy.

But Edward was anxious about Cassie. 'Where will she go now?'

'There's only one place I *can* go,' Cassie said. The railway van was out of the question because of balaclava man; and she wouldn't feel safe alone in that enormous barn. So that left Edward's house.

How numb and confused he looks! Cassie thought.

'I'll feel quite safe,' she said. 'No one will expect a girl to be hiding in an empty house where someone's just died. Besides, the front and back doors have massive bolts.'

'And the windows are all stuck,' Edward said.

Molly, watching as she always did, thought to herself, *He wants to be there, with her.*

So Cassie went to Edward's house as darkness was falling. Edward had wanted them all to go with her, but the others pointed out that a crowd would attract attention. So, alone, Cassie locked herself in, kept clear of windows, and went thankfully to bed without switching on any lights.

No outside prowler tried to open doors; no hooded intruder crept stealthily up the stairs; no dark watcher stood motionless in the shadows of the landing. Everything that troubled Cassie was inside her head.

She passed a troubled and sleepless night, full of tangled and scary uncertainties. But as daylight filled the sky she fell into a deep sleep – and woke later to the sound of someone downstairs. Edward had come to see that she was all right. He called out to her so that she wouldn't be scared. Then he burst into her bedroom, looking eager and anxious.

Cassie sat up in bed feeling washed out and grubby, as if she'd been beaten up. She was pleased to see Edward. *My half-hero*, she thought sleepily.

❧

That evening, Group Captain Rayburn was about to enjoy a gin and tonic in the officers' mess when he spied Hilda Pritt striding among the tables towards him.

She wasted no words. 'Your Crossley,' she said. 'Can I borrow it? Just for an hour or two.'

He glared indignantly at her. He never allowed anyone to drive his beloved Crossley. 'No, you jolly well can't!' he said. 'You've got a nerve!'

'Don't be a spoilsport, Teddy,' she said. 'I don't want it for a jaunt. It's part of the investigation.'

He thought for a moment. 'All right! But *I'll* drive.'

They left the mess together and walked quickly across to where the handsome royal-blue Crossley was parked beside number one hangar. It had been raining on and off all day, and they lowered their heads against the gusty wind. Then Hilda started to run, reached the car first, and slipped into the driver's seat before Teddy Rayburn got there.

He was furious. He wrenched open the car door and shouted. 'I *say*! Get out of there, Hilda! You can't do that. This is *my car*!'

'Don't stand there making an ass of yourself,' Hilda said calmly. 'Come round the other side and get in. Or I'll drive off and leave you there. And you'll get soaked!'

He could see she meant business. As he climbed into the passenger seat, he said, 'You've got a damned cheek, Hilda!'

'I know,' she said sweetly, and pressed her right foot on the accelerator and her left hand on his knee. (*To put him in a better mood*, she said to herself.)

'Where are we going?' (He was still cross.)

'Ely. To see an English teacher.'

'Dame Whatsit?'

'Yes. Lily – Dame Lily.'

'Why?' he asked. (*She drives a car just like she flies a plane*, he thought. *Skilfully, gracefully, attentive to everything. Mind, body and machine in perfect coordination.*)

'Because,' Hilda said, 'there's something about Dame Lily that *just doesn't fit.*'

Hilda drove the Crossley to Ely, slowly past St Dorothea's Boarding School, and on to the entrance next-door. They studied the wrought iron gates and the drive that led through thick trees to Dame Lily's house.

'Plenty of money there,' Teddy murmured.

'*And* they own the farm next door,' Hilda said. She'd found that out by talking to a farm worker in a pub. 'Let's have a peek at it.'

After Dame Lily's house the town gave way to open fields, and less than a mile further on they could see a farmhouse. It stood a long way back from the road and was derelict, with windows bricked up. A sign at the roadside said *Stump Farm*.

'Perfect for hiding someone,' Hilda said.

'Yes,' Teddy Rayburn said, 'but Tittipat's chaps would have investigated it.'

Hilda was not so sure. Mr Tittipat probably didn't employ her methods.

There were muddy tyre tracks on the road. *Lots* of

tyre tracks, made by cars, not tractors. Why, Hilda wondered as they set off back to the airbase, would anyone in a car need to drive to an abandoned farmhouse? Lots of times.

Cassie's second night alone in Edward's house was different. She slept deeply all night. But, as dawn was breaking, she had a vivid and troubling dream about the mild old man who'd been on the beach at Hunstanton, with his dog. And his beard.

In her dream he stared silently at her, and his long silky beard *waved about* – and then pointed directly at her as she walked by.

She awoke with a start and sat up to ponder the dream. She thought about it all that day – Sunday – and the next day too. There was nothing strange about an old man with a beard. The baffling thing was that the beard had *moved* – and seemed to be pointing at her.

Late in the afternoon, when she was waiting for the others to come home, it suddenly made sense to Cassie, and she understood why the night intruder with the gun had had a distorted chin under his balaclava.

I must warn Dame Lily, she said to herself.

That was why she went to Ely. She tried phoning first but nobody answered. So, because it was grey and gusty, and it kept coming on to rain, she caught the evening bus.

The others, arriving at the barn, found a note from Cassie explaining where she had gone. But not why.

Edward was filled with alarm (it was intuitive, nothing he could explain) and insisted on setting off at once to follow her, on his bike. Which he did.

The others had to go home for their bikes and to tell Mrs Barnes and Mrs Murfitt (as vaguely as they could get away with) why they were going for an unplanned evening cycle ride.

By the time they got away. Edward was about three miles ahead of them.

34
Friend or Foe?

Cassie hesitated on the stone step, hoping it would be Dame Lily who came to the door. She'd always felt a little in awe of Sir Tristram. She pulled the brass handle and heard the bell jangling inside.

Hmm, she thought, for it was Sir Tristram who opened the door. Cassie murmured that she needed to talk to Dame Lily, and was she at home, please?

'Yes, of course, my dear. Come in,' Sir Tristram said. She saw at once that he was startled. *Of course!* she thought. *He was used to* girls *coming to the house.* There had always been girls a-plenty in need of a few minutes with his sister. But boys hardly at all. Never, probably.

Sir Tristram adjusted his language. 'Follow me, old chap.'

He led Cassie into the drawing room with a large bay window at the front of the house. She was familiar with it because she'd been there with Uncle Peter. For tea.

Nothing to alarm her there – but the sight of Dame Lily came as a shock. As her English teacher laid down her sewing beside her table lamp, Cassie saw how ill and haggard she looked. She frowned as she stared at Cassie, as if she was confused.

Cassie hastily explained. 'I'm *Cassie*,' she said brightly.

This seemed to upset Dame Lily even more. She looked quickly at her brother, for reassurance Cassie supposed. 'Cassie?'

'Yes, Cassie Covington. I ran away. Then I cut off my hair. And I'm dressed as a boy.'

She felt foolish, explaining all this. How silly it sounded when you put it into words. But Dame Lily fell back into her armchair. *Why is she shaking?* Cassie thought.

'Tristram dear,' Dame Lily said to her brother. 'Do you think you could leave us alone for a few minutes? Make us some tea, would you? Be a darling.'

I expect he's used to that, Cassie thought. But Sir Tristram shook his head. 'I think I'd better stay. Why did you run away, my dear?'

Cassie turned to him. 'Because I was scared. I found some people in our house, searching. And I . . .'

'Security people, I dare say,' he said. 'Your uncle told us a little about his work, you know.'

'*And* I didn't want to be taken away. And put into an orphanage.'

She looked at Dame Lily in search of the old sympathy, that unfailing understanding that every girl at St Dorothea's had found in her when they needed it.

But Dame Lily seemed unable to speak. She looked nervously from her brother to Cassie and back again. Repeatedly.

'The reason I've come is to tell you about Sergeant Prater,' she went on. 'He came looking for me – with a *gun*! He's a bad man!'

Their reaction was not what she'd expected. They exchanged anxious looks – looks that meant more than Cassie understood.

'And we don't believe Uncle Peter is really dead,' she added weakly.

'*We?*' Sir Tristram said. 'Who's *we?*'

Oh! Cassie thought. That was not the response she'd expected. Sympathy perhaps. Amused disbelief even. But not that question, so sharply asked.

An instinct of secrecy prompted her then, a tiny doubt, a guardedness.

She lied.

'Me and my teddy,' she said. She turned to Dame Lily. '*You* remember him.' (Clearly, Dame Lily didn't.)

'I think,' Sir Tristram said slowly, 'this is a matter for Stumpers.'

Stumpers? What was he talking about?

'No, Tristram, please,' said Dame Lily.

'Come, child,' Sir Tristram said to Cassie. 'You were quite right. Your uncle *is* alive. We will take you to see him.'

So why was it *fear* that Cassie felt as he approached her? Why this growing doubt? Why wasn't she overjoyed? Or even relieved?

'Come, Lily.' It was an order to his sister. A command.

'But how do you know where Uncle Peter is?' she said to Dame Lily. 'Has he been hiding here?'

'In a manner of speaking,' Dame Lily said quietly.

It made some sense, that Uncle Peter might have gone to his old lady friend for safety. So Cassie allowed hope to overrule her uneasiness – and, as a result of that hesitation, almost before she was aware of it the three of them were leaving the house.

Sir Tristram was holding her left arm, leading her to the car that was parked in the drive. On the other side Dame Lily held her hand. If the car had been further away Cassie's doubts might have clarified themselves. And she might have had time to pull herself free and make a dash for it. But the car was close to the doorstep.

'You drive,' Sir Tristram said to his sister. He pushed Cassie into the back seat and got in beside her.

That was when Cassie understood that she was a prisoner. And that she'd left it too late to get away.

Edward saw it all.

He had arrived only minutes after Cassie, having first raced up the wrong drive, to the school next door. Angry with himself, he tried the next entrance – and was just in time to see Cassie almost frog-marched to the car.

He ducked in the bushes as the car passed by him. Darkness was beginning to fall and in the half-light Cassie's face was white and frightened. It was like a moment in one of his dreams. He – and everything around him – were strangely still. Even the moving car and the gusting wind were seized by a quiet remoteness. The strangest thing of all was that none of it surprised him.

His first idea was to cycle after the car. But that, he told himself, would be useless. He would never be able to keep up with it.

Then he remembered walking past the front of the house on the night of the play, and there had been a man using a telephone in the front room. He raced across the drive, slowing to a walk as he approached the front door. A light had been left on in the front room, and he could see the phone standing on a table in the window.

He didn't hesitate. He tried the front door, found it was unlocked, and went inside. He wasted no time taking in the details of the entrance hall. He went quickly towards the room on his left, peered cautiously in, and then crossed to the telephone.

He lifted the receiver and dialled the number which Hilda had given them, and which he had carefully memorised. The call did not go through the exchange. A direct contact was mysteriously made, almost immediately, and a voice said, '*Yes?*'

'*Sleeping Beauty*,' Edward said. Then, 'Cassie's been kidnapped.'

'Where are you?'

There was a white disc on the telephone, with a number on it. 'Ely 791,' Edward said.

Then the weird dream that Edward seemed to be in took on a new momentum – brutally, from behind, by a strong square man with a waxed and pointed beard, who had crept up on him. He put a gun to the side of Edward's head and with his other hand pulled him violently back from the phone.

Molly, Abigail and Adam approached the main gate just in time to see a car leaving and driving away. They were not close enough to see who was inside it.

'We should go after it!' Abigail said as they dismounted. Molly agreed, but Adam said they should have a look at the house too.

They divided jobs without discussion. That's what happens when people have a shared history. There's less need to argue.

'We won't be able to keep up with that car,' Molly said.

'But you might see where it's going,' Adam pointed out.

So they left him there, and he pushed his bike among the bushes, and set off along the darkening drive. The leather saddle on Adam's bike had hardened with age; it had been like sitting astride a bit of carved wood. His legs trembled, his balls were numb, and his knees felt shaky.

Someone had closed the curtains of the big bay window but he could see that there was a light in the room. Then he saw that the front door was ajar – and he stepped cautiously inside.

The hall was in darkness, and from the other side of a door on his left Adam could hear a voice. 'Listen, you little runt! You got away from me before but if you try anything this time I'll blow your brains out.'

The voice was low and cold, its intention clear. Adam knew with a sudden understanding that he had moved out of ordinary life and into a different place, where there were different rules, and different ways of thinking. This world was cold, black and white, and edged with danger – and it was always there, just out of sight.

But Adam also found that there was a part of him that matched it, a readiness, a quick-thinking, an anger perfectly controlled. Nobody – not just Edward – *nobody* should ever be spoken to like that, with such cruel words, with such menace. No one in the world, *ever*.

He knew without looking that the man had a gun. He guessed too that he was facing the door – so that if Adam entered the room he would be in the line of fire.

So he slipped back outside, and hurried round to the back of the house, knowing with perfect certainty that there would be a back door, or a side door, another entrance of some kind.

And he found it.

He was in a kind of scullery, with ironing boards and brooms, and two huge white kitchen sinks. Through that he went, quickly and stealthily – and found himself in a kitchen, then a dark passage. At the end of it was a room with a light on, and an open door . . .

– and that man's voice talking cruelty and anger.

But not just cruelty and anger. There was uncertainty too. Adam, with the sharpened understanding of this shadow-world that he found himself in, knew at once that the speaker *was not sure what he should do.*

Abigail and Molly did not have to cycle far. In the last of the grey half-light they saw the car turn left off the main road. They could see its rear lights. When they reached the place where it had turned, there was a rough and muddy farm track leading as straight as an arrow to a distant building, bare and stark in the empty landscape.

A farmhouse. An ancient wooden sign told them that it was *Stump Farm*.

They heard the distant slamming of car doors, and prepared to set off along the track.

'Wait a minute,' Molly said. The roadside ditch had recently been cleared and deepened, and uneven mounds of chalky clay had been dug out. Molly found a fist-sized lump of chalk and took it over to the signpost. The chalk was wet and crumbly, but she managed to write *CASSIE* on the sign – messily – with an arrow underneath pointing to the farmhouse.

Abigail waited, holding both bikes. 'We don't *know* she's there.'

'Just in case she is,' Molly said.

They splashed and bumped their way along the farm track towards the darkening house. The moon was hidden, and a wide level cloud like a mudbank covered half the sky.

When they reached the empty car parked outside the house, everything they saw had the shape and form of familiarity. And as they crept cautiously towards the front door and saw that it was not properly shut, they might have been able to convince themselves that this was no more than a prank – a bit of childish prowling.

But once they'd slipped inside, they found nothing familiar, nothing they could recognise. This place assaulted their eyes with a kind of lunacy, and shocked their brains into confusion.

The house was a deception. As far as they'd been able to see from the outside, it was an ordinary farmhouse, like a hundred others in the Fens. But inside it was not a house at all.

It was an emptiness, a huge emptiness, an enormous hollow cube, with no rooms. There were no inside walls. No doors, no furniture, no fireplaces. Windows were bricked up and the upstairs floor joists were supported by thick wooden posts. When they looked up, they saw that in fact there was *no* upstairs. There were no rooms up there either, and they could see right through to the wooden boards of the attic floor at the top of the house.

In those boards there was an open trapdoor. And a massive ladder – they'd never seen one so long – led to it, two floors up, dizzyingly distant.

There was a light up there, in the attic above that trapdoor, and some of it spilled faintly down. It was because of this that they were able to see. They could hear voices, up there, above the open trapdoor.

Abigail took Molly's arm and they drew closer to one another.

For this vast and cavernous space was occupied. Someone had built a monstrous bonfire, inert and waiting, a mountain of timber stacked so dizzily that it reached the first-floor joists and continued up where the bedrooms should have been. It was broad at the base, filling the middle of the floor, tapering to an uneven summit, and enveloping the big support posts so that they too were part of it. There were bits of old furniture, dried-up rain barrels, dozens of long floorboards, old fence posts, the trunks of trees, and an entire hay wagon upended with its wheels facing grotesquely outwards and its shafts reaching up into where the upstairs ought to have been. And nestled among these objects were a thousand and one broken fragments of long-forgotten thrown-away rubbish, an accumulation of years.

It was not unwanted rubbish casually thrown into a pile. It had been *constructed*, carefully built for a purpose. It was entirely wooden, and tinder-dry – a labour of lunacy. *Cruel* and *deliberate* lunacy they realised, for around the base were loose bundles of dry straw. Beneath the straw were twists of crunched-up newspapers.

'We could just go,' Abigail whispered.

Molly nodded.

Yes, we could leave at once, she thought. But they both knew they wouldn't. Once inside that door, they had passed a point of no return.

Barely five minutes earlier Cassie too had seen the extraordinary bonfire stacked inside the naked house. But she hadn't taken it in. Its weirdness – and its sinister Guy Fawkes malevolence – had not made its full impact on her.

This was because she was still buoyed up with hope, a confused and doubting half-belief that she was – she really *was* – going to see Uncle Peter.

During the short car ride she'd said, 'Are you really taking me to him?'

Dame Lily's brother had said, 'Yes, my dear, of course we are.'

She thought Dame Lily, driving, was about to speak – but Sir Tristram shut her up. 'Don't be foolish, Lily,' he'd said.

So as they entered the house Cassie's heart was thumping wildly in her chest. Was it fear? Or hope?

Up the ladder they made her go, to the high and distant attic, Dame Lily first, then Cassie, then Sir Tristram panting hard with the effort. The trapdoor was pushed open, a dim lightbulb was switched on, and she scrambled clumsily in.

This is what she *saw* in the shadows as she straightened up:

~ a big dim attic space, a wide wooden floor, dusty; and the steep sloping undersides of roof tiles.

~ Uncle Peter (*was* it Uncle Peter?) sprawled on the floor, blinking as his eyes grew accustomed to the light.

~ a rope binding him to an upright post at his back; his arms bound tight against the sides of his body; another rope around his ankles.

~ a piece of cloth stuffed into his mouth and held there by a rag knotted tightly around his lower face.

~ another length of rope tight around his neck, so that he would be throttled if he allowed his head to fall forward.

And this is what she *felt*:

~ relief at first, a wonderful, wonderful joy and thankfulness that Uncle Peter wasn't after all dead and buried. *Thank you, thank you, God!*

– distress and concern at the state he was in, that he looked so ill and so unlike himself.

~ fear for herself.

~ anger, a growing outrage that anyone could do such things.

And this is what she *understood*:

~ that they had wanted Uncle Peter to reveal what he knew about the coming invasion of France.

~ that he had so far held out.

~ that now they planned to use her as a further persuasion.

~ and, whether or not he finally told them what

they wanted to know, they would both be disposed of in the end.

Those things did not come into her mind in that order; nor did they take as long to happen as it takes to read about them. It took no more than a few seconds for her to see what was to be seen, to feel what she felt, and to understand what it meant.

Yet she was perfectly calm. *I'm perfectly calm*, she thought to herself in surprise.

Edward stood, petrified, facing the bearded man with the gun. Again, a second time! The door was close behind him but he knew he would be shot before he could reach it.

'Where are the others?' Sergeant Prater demanded.

'On their way,' Edward lied. But his voice had come out as an inaudible croak. So he said it again, more firmly. 'They're on their way.'

'I don't believe you, you little scrap. God, I hate kids!'

There was an ivory box on the table by the telephone. Sergeant Prater lifted the lid, took out a cigarette, and put it between his lips. *How*, Edward wondered, *is he going to take out a match and strike it with one hand? He'd have to put down the gun.* But Sergeant Prater, still holding the gun, pulled a lighter from his pocket and flicked it into flame.

But he had no time to light his cigarette. Edward saw a shape materialise silently in the shadows of another door, behind Sergeant Prater. As he realised who it was, his eyes widened and his face lit up.

Adam moved quietly forward, and Sergeant Prater – totally unaware – said sneeringly to Edward, 'Stop pulling faces! You needn't think I'm going to fall for that old trick!'

So Edward tried to cancel his facial expression and pretend that he was still frightened (except that it *wasn't* a pretence because he was).

'You fooled me once before but you're not going to get away again.'

'Actually,' Adam said from behind him, 'you're wrong about that. He *is*.'

Sergeant Prater almost jumped. He swung round to see who was behind him, who had spoken those taunting words.

'Edward! *Run!*'

But Edward didn't run. He wanted to stay with Adam. Together they could do anything, he thought. And what would happen if he left Adam to the mercy of this man?

Sergeant Prater, still shaken, could not simultaneously point his gun in two opposite directions. He was brutal, and he was disciplined – but he could not alter the geography of that room. Either one or the other of those boys was going to get away.

Adam tried again. 'Go and find the others!' he said to Edward. 'I *mean* it.'

This time Edward took him at his word. In an instant

he had reached the door into the hall and raced out into the darkness.

He heard Adam shout. *'They went left!'*

Then there was a gunshot, and the sound of smashed glass falling.

Enjoying a mug of cocoa in the mess at the airbase, Hilda saw Group Captain Rayburn striding towards her.

'Come on!' he said quietly. 'Someone's phoned.'

She knew immediately what he meant. Someone had phoned the security number. Without a second's hesitation she followed him outside to his car. This time he intended to drive it himself.

As they raced towards the exit she said, 'Who?'

'They don't know. A boy, probably.'

'Where was he?'

'He gave a phone number. Ely 791. Tittipat's staff will be trying to identify it right now.'

But Hilda didn't need to identify it. She'd done her homework. 'I *knew* I was right!' she said. 'I looked it up, just in case. It's Dame Lily's number!'

They went through the Fens at a roaring speed, and Hilda observed with interest how Teddy Rayburn drove his car – managing with skill and exactness to stay by a single hair's breadth on the safe side of recklessness. Well, he *would* be a good driver, she thought. Of course he would! In the early years of the War he'd been an outstanding fighter pilot, going up daily during the Battle of Britain and somehow surviving those perils. Handling machines at speed came naturally to him.

When he was four and she was ten he'd been a sad little boy. But, she thought to herself, sad little boys can grow up to be heroic. This one had.

They reached the outskirts of Ely, and in no time at all the Crossley's tyres were crunching the gravel on Sir Tristram's drive.

When Uncle Peter saw Cassie he groaned.

She rushed over and knelt beside him on the dusty floorboards. As she struggled to dislodge the gag that was stuffed in his mouth, his eyes stared up at her, seeming to burn in his filthy unshaven face. He tried to speak, but it seemed that he'd forgotten how to do it. He made a horrible rasping noise. Then he glanced to one side of him and Cassie saw there was a bucket of water and an enamel mug. She dipped the mug in the water and held it for him to drink.

There was a good deal of dribbling and spilling, and another bout of coughing. But at last he was able to say something.

Uncle Peter had been in danger often enough to know that explanations were a waste of time. People always wanted to ask questions and work out what had happened, and why it had happened. It was natural that they should do that – but it was always pointless, and usually dangerous.

He went straight to the point. With the few words that he could manage to get out clearly he said simply, 'You have to get away. *Now!* Do anything you have to, but *get away from these two*!'

Cassie turned her head. 'How could you do this to him?' she said quietly. 'I thought you loved him.'

Was Dame Lily distressed? Or frightened? Ashamed perhaps? Cassie couldn't tell. 'He wanted to *marry* you!' she said.

Uncle Peter said something inaudible. She turned back to him, put her face close to his, and paid attention. 'Don't waste words. *Get out!*' His breath smelt, his body smelt, his clothes stank.

Dame Lily made an appeal to her brother. 'Trissy!' she said. (She'd called him that when he was six, and she was two.) 'Please . . .'

'Lily,' he said sharply. 'This is no time for weakness. If you can't bear it, go – and leave everything to me.'

His sister took him at his word. She moved to the open trapdoor and stepped onto the top rungs of the ladder.

&

Back at Dame Lily's house, this is what happened.

Adam was about to make a dive for Sergeant Prater's legs, hoping to bring him to the ground. But the Sergeant was a hard and experienced fighter. He anticipated Adam's move and fired his revolver directly into the lampshade immediately above Adam's head.

The light in the room dimmed and broken glass showered and rang over Adam's head and shoulders. It was an uncanny feeling, utterly unexpected, and he just stood in the middle of the room, taken aback and confused.

'Sit down!' Sergeant Prater snapped.

Adam looked at him, puzzled. *Sit down?* The tone of voice was sharp and menacing, but the words were the kind of thing that people said if you were at an interview, or a tea party. (*Do* sit down!)

Then his thinking switched itself on again – and he saw at once why this gunman wanted him to sit. It would take a fraction of a second longer for a seated person to leap into action than it would a person already standing.

He turned slowly, considering and choosing carefully where he would sit. Then he lowered himself onto the chair beside Dame Lily's table and lamp, and faced Sergeant Prater. There was a pause, and then Adam said brightly, 'Well, what are we going to talk about?'

'Who are you?' Sergeant Prater said.

'I'm Adam Swales. We're looking for Cassie's uncle, Mr Peter Dinsdale.'

Adam was not as casual as he seemed. He was focused on Sergeant Prater's face – and he saw and understood the tiny flicker of doubt at his use of the word *we*.

He slid his right hand down the wall behind his chair, out of sight, searching.

'I could do with a boy like you in my lot,' Sergeant Prater said. And Adam thought, *What nonsense is this?*

'You've got guts. I can see that.'

Adam's hand found the electric socket where the table lamp was plugged in. And at that moment they both heard the wheels of a car crunching the gravel outside on the drive.

Sergeant Prater pointed his gun at Adam with a new resoluteness. The gesture meant: do nothing, say nothing.

Adam waited, his secret finger on the switch.

The engine was turned off. Two car doors slammed. They heard footsteps approaching the front of the house.

Sergeant Prater slipped behind the drawing-room door, his gun still pointed at Adam.

And Adam, with perfect timing, switched off the table lamp and plunged the room into darkness – but only *after* he had been briefly seen by Hilda and her companion.

❧

'Let's explore,' Abigail whispered.

Molly followed her and they crept quietly round the base of the rubbish stack. They picked their way slowly because the floor was in darkness and littered with fragments of wood and rubbish. All the time they could hear the rustle of voices, someone talking at the top of that ladder, in the attic.

'Do you think she's up there?' Molly said.

She probably was, they thought – on the other hand this might have nothing at all to do with Cassie, or *them*.

Abigail suddenly gripped Molly's arm and pointed

242

up. A woman's foot was feeling its way towards a rung at the top of the ladder. Once it was safely placed, the other foot followed with a similar action. Then, slowly, they began the descent.

Molly and Abigail stared as if they'd been turned to stone by a creature from mythology. A woman – foreshortened – began to descend the ladder, slowly, but with more confidence than those early steps had suggested.

She was halfway down before the girls had time to realise that they needed to hide.

'*Who are you!* What are you doing here?'

They could have said *We're looking for Cassie,* but they didn't. Molly was sure she was the one who'd been spotted. Abigail was further round the base of the bonfire, probably out of sight. So, in a sudden sensible instinct, Molly pushed Abigail further into the darkness while she herself stepped forward. (They'd done this a hundred times at school, one owning up to protect the other.)

She didn't speak because she couldn't think what to say. The woman reached the bottom of the ladder with surprising speed and grabbed Molly by the shoulders. 'Who are you?'

Our lives are full of moments when we might have done one thing but we do another without knowing quite why. Molly could easily have broken free and got away. This woman wasn't young, and not especially strong. But she didn't. She stayed there, at a loss for words, but knowing with perfect clarity that she couldn't abandon Abigail.

'Tristram!' the woman shouted. *'Tristram!* You had better come down. There's someone here!'

Abigail, crouching in the shadows, saw a face appear in the square trapdoor above them, distant and small. And the next moment Sir Tristram was descending the ladder. He'd gone up it slowly, and breathing heavily. But he came down swiftly, almost like a trapeze artist in a circus, one-handed, and his feet moving nimbly.

One-handed because in his other hand he held a gun.

Abigail watched in appalled fascination as he reached the bottom and pointed the gun at Molly. And Molly – much to her disgust later when she remembered it – put her hands up as they always did in films.

But her instinct to keep Abigail hidden had been a good one. Slowly because of the unseen rubbish on the floor, Abigail crept quietly round the other side of the bonfire until she was almost back where they'd started. There was a short thick plank of wood at her feet. She picked it up, and crept further round.

'Up!' Sir Tristram commanded. 'Up that ladder! Now!' He gestured at Molly with his gun, shepherding her towards the bottom of the ladder.

But Molly refused to budge. A stubbornness unexpectedly took her over, and she just stood there, shaking her head.

At that moment Dame Lily yelled, *'Tristram!'*

She'd seen Abigail, who had crept into view

unnoticed, holding the plank of wood like a blunt ungainly javelin aimed at Sir Tristram's wrist, the hand that held the gun.

If he'd seen Abigail, he would certainly have had time to lower his hand so that her javelin-thrust missed. Or he might even have fired the gun into Molly's chest. But neither of those things happened because at that moment there was a movement just inside the door – and it was there that Sir Tristram looked instead.

Edward had slipped inside like a grey shadow and was standing there with a worried look on his face – and then one of disbelief as he took in what he was seeing.

In that instant when everyone was staring at Edward, Abigail launched her weapon, a great end-on blow that caught Sir Tristram's gun-hand as he turned slightly towards Edward. He yelled in pain, and swore savagely.

The gun fell to the floor as he used his good hand to cradle his injured wrist. He hugged it to his chest with his head lifted and an expression of agony on his face. Dame Lily released Molly and hurried over to her brother. He collapsed to his knees and she crouched beside him.

Edward came further in, mystified. Abigail searched for the gun but couldn't find it among the shadowy floor rubbish.

'Is Cassie here?' Edward whispered.

Molly indicated the ladder. 'We think she's up there,' she said.

In the sudden darkness of Dame Lily's sitting room, Adam had slipped quickly sideways, away from the chair. As he moved he yelled, '*He's behind the door!*'

Sergeant Prater had no time to shoot. Group Captain Rayburn, whose thinking in action had always been swift and accurate, slammed the door back hard against the wall, smashing it into Sergeant Prater and knocking the gun out of his hand.

They were all in darkness. Adam heard the sounds of a struggle and a good deal of heavy breathing. By the time he'd found the switch and put the lamp back on, Sergeant Prater had escaped and Rayburn had raced off in pursuit.

'*Adam!* Are you all right?' It was Hilda.

He wanted to grin at her, like a war hero in a film. He couldn't manage the grin but he got the words more or less right. 'Of course I am!' he said. She stooped to pick up the gun that Sergeant Prater had dropped.

The Group Captain came back. 'I lost him. The house is a maze of passages. The blighter could be anywhere.'

He faced Adam. 'I say! You're a cool customer.'

Yes, he is! Hilda thought. 'Where are the others?' she asked.

'I don't know,' Adam said, 'but I know which direction they took.'

Another car arrived at Stump Farm ahead of them, carrying Mr Tittipat and some of his team, all armed. Silently they surrounded the house. Mr Tittipat and one other approached the door, with Hilda, Teddy Rayburn and Adam close behind.

That part of it was over very quickly. Dame Lily, weeping silently, and Sir Tristram clutching his shattered wrist, were held at gunpoint. Very little was said.

Edward wanted to be the first to climb the ladder but this was not allowed. Mr Tittipat sent up one of his men.

'You see, I was right,' Hilda said cheerfully to Mr Tittipat. 'About Dame Lily.'

He gave her a look of such chilling contempt that she was silenced utterly. Molly, who hated being snubbed, tucked her hand in Hilda's arm and whispered, 'Take no notice.'

After what seemed like an age Uncle Peter appeared at the trapdoor above their heads. But he seemed almost unable to put his weight on his legs. He clung for dear life to the edge of the trapdoor while his feet found a rung at the top of the ladder. Then, with unbearable slowness, he began the journey down to the ground, shakily, tremulously. From time to time his legs failed to hold his weight and he was saved from falling only because he held on with his hands. One of the men climbed up to meet him and that helped a little.

It seemed to take an hour. But at last he reached the ground safely and slowly turned himself around to see who was there. That was when his eyes fell on four children, two girls and two boys. This confused him utterly. 'Who are you?' he said in a voice that scratched like chalk on a blackboard.

'We're Cassie's friends,' Abigail said.

They didn't quite catch his reply. But it might have been: 'Friends? Cassie doesn't *have* any friends!'

Then he turned to Mr Tittipat. 'Titty, old chap! Trust you to be here.'

What did *that* mean? Molly sensed that these two men had their own secret history.

Mr Tittipat turned to the man who'd been in the attic. 'Anything?' he asked.

'No, sir. Only the girl, and she's all right.'

'Can you make it to the car?' Mr Tittipat said to Uncle Peter. He turned to the children. 'A couple of my staff will stay. They'll keep an eye on you. I'll send another car shortly. And don't touch anything!'

He turned to the Group Captain. 'We'll take Sir Tristram in our car. Can you take his sister in yours?'

'It will be a pleasure!' Teddy Rayburn said. 'Come on, Hilda. You sit in the back with a gun at her head.'

Suddenly the four of them were alone. They heard

Mr Tittipat giving orders outside; then doors slamming, and the sound of cars being driven away. (*If this had been a film*, Molly thought, *this was the moment – in this unexpected pause in the action – when an owl would hoot.*)

It felt somehow wrong, unfinished, to be left there like that. No one had said *thank you*, no one had said *well done*. No one had behaved as if anything of importance had happened. Mr Tittipat had shown no interest in Cassie, or in what had happened to her. Molly already knew that he had no interest in children. But it was worse than that: he hardly seemed even to *see* them unless they were forced upon his attention.

And it felt wrong that the two men who'd stayed behind were dressed in ordinary clothes. They ought to have been soldiers in uniform, or police perhaps. Clearly their job wasn't to keep an eye on the children. *We might just as well be invisible*, Molly thought. One of the men lit a cigarette, and then they both went back outside – and not a word said.

And why hadn't Cassie come down? Was something wrong?

As soon as they were left alone Edward set off up that enormous ladder – past where the bedroom floors would have been if there had been an upstairs – up and beyond to the very top of the building, with the great stacked heap of wood beside him all the way up.

Adam made a move towards the ladder but Abigail held him back. 'Shouldn't we go with him?' he said.

Both girls shook their heads and Adam – uncomprehending – shrugged and stood back.

Cassie, kneeling on the rough attic floor, saw Edward's white face appear through the trapdoor space. 'Come and see!' she said.

He climbed carefully up and in, then crossed to where she knelt, holding a book. It was not like Uncle Peter's book, this one. It was smaller and fatter, more like a five-year diary. They huddled close as she showed him.

'I found it here,' she said.

'What's in it?' Edward whispered.

'There's no need to whisper,' Cassie said.

But he continued to whisper. They both whispered. Everything around them – every shadowy sinister thing – seemed to *compel* them to whisper.

Edward took the book and saw almost at once that it was a list of everything that Dame Lily and her brother had done since the start of the War. There were no blots, no crossings-out, no scribbles. Everything was recorded in neat, clear writing. Cassie shoved it inside her shirt.

'Where's my uncle?' Cassie said.

'They've taken him away in a car. To Molly's guest house, I think.'

The three downstairs were waiting. They felt oppressed by this weird non-house with its gargantuan ready-laid fire. 'Let's find the gun Sir Whatsit dropped,' Abigail said. Anything to drive away the dark unhappy stillness of this place.

They began to search among the litter of the floor. But it was too dark to see clearly – and they didn't notice until too late a figure creeping quietly round from the other side of the wood mountain.

There must have been a back door that none of them had noticed, and as they straightened they saw that a man had come in, with his head held unnaturally high and a strange forward-pointing beard.

Adam knew at once that they were in danger.

But Sergeant Prater had no weapon. There *was* danger, but it was not the risk of being shot. The danger was in that stubborn thrusting beard perhaps, or in his strangely burning eyes.

This gloomy cavernous place seemed to steal their words, to oppress speech and stifle it. Even Sergeant Prater said nothing when he saw them. Instead, he stooped silently down, as if searching for something.

Three things happened very quickly. One was that flames were suddenly crackling and leaping where Sergeant Prater had bent down. The second was that he made a dash towards the front door, pile-driving straight through them so that Abigail and Adam were knocked violently sideways. Finally, as he went past the bottom of the ladder, he grabbed it and yanked it violently forward so that the top slipped out of the open trapdoor, fell sideways, and collapsed onto the waiting bonfire.

Above their heads the trapdoor fell shut with a solid thunk.

In the attic the lightbulb flickered. Edward and Cassie, crouching together like two beggar children in a Victorian picture, looked up in unison and stared at the trapdoor. Edward hurried over to it and tried to open it from above. Cassie followed. They found there was no handle and it was impossible to get a grip on the edge.

They struggled and heaved, but the only result was broken fingernails.

'The others are down there,' Edward said. 'They'll get help.'

He had to stay calm. It was his task to reassure Cassie that everything would be all right. And she was thinking they were going to be trapped up there for ages and she hoped the light wouldn't go out. But she said nothing because there was no point in giving her half-hero something else to worry about.

Outside, there was a gunshot. The two men left behind by Mr Tittipat had been watching the door, and they saw Sergeant Prater leaving the house and making a dash for freedom. They went in pursuit.

This was unfortunate for the five left inside.

The flames spread with amazing speed through the paper and straw that had been laid there. The wood was so dry that each tiny fragment was ignited at once and the fire exploded almost instantly into a furnace. Almost before the three could take in the enormity of what might happen, a thousand writhing flames were leaping up towards the underside of the attic boards, red and roaring, wrapping and weaving around the wooden support posts with a fierce and terrifying intensity.

In such an enclosed space it grew unbearably hot almost immediately.

'The ladder!' Adam shouted.

Upstairs Edward and Cassie heard the crackling of the flames. It began to get hot as they struggled with the trapdoor. Delicate wisps of smoke threaded sweetly through the gaps in the floorboards, wavering, like little baby ghosts.

'The fire brigade will come,' one of them said. But they both knew it might not arrive in time.

Downstairs, the three struggled with the ladder and dragged it towards the door. They knew that if they tried to use it inside to reach Cassie and Edward it would be burnt to cinders in minutes. But outside there might be some way of saving them.

With nowhere to escape to, the heat and smoke of the fire built up inside the hollow house. It is never easy to manoeuvre a long straight ladder, but the three of them – frightened by the intensifying heat and coughing in the poisonous smoke – succeeded at last in getting it round the base of the fire, through the front door, and out into the night. And how cool it felt out there after the terrible heat inside! How good it was to breathe fresh clean air!

They heard gunshots, away at the edge of the field. And shouts.

'Come on!' Edward said.

Has he thought of something? Cassie wondered. He moved away from the trapdoor to the outer edge of the attic where he had to crouch low under the steeply sloping roof. Then he began to thump with his fists on the undersides of the tiles over his head.

'What are you doing?' Cassie yelled.

'We have to break through!'

He'll never break those tiles with his bare hands, she thought. The tiles were brick-solid and brick-rough.

'*Shoes!*' she yelled at him. She tore off her shoes, shoved her hands inside them, and used them like gloves to hammer away at the tiles.

Quickly Edward followed suit. It was awkward, but at least they weren't sandpapering their hands down to the raw blood.

Side by side they worked, desperately bashing at the roof above their heads. Cassie's whole body was sticky with sweat and just to get her head out into the night air would be a relief. *But it's a long way down,* she thought.

The tiles were laid on parallel wooden laths. At first they thought they were nailed to them. But they weren't. Each tile had a wooden peg which latched over its lath. And each was weighted down by others overlapping it. So, once they'd smashed through the first few, the others were easier. They were able simply to lift each tile off its lath and send it clattering noisily down until it slid off the roof and hurtled into space.

Then the light went out. In the blackness they jostled, nudged, felt for each other.

One person could not have carried the ladder at all. Two might have managed it, with difficulty. But the three of them were able to hurry round to the outside of the farmhouse and raise it.

But it was not long enough. The top of the ladder did not reach the top of the wall.

It was a question of geometry. They had to shift the base closer to the house so that the ladder was almost vertical. This would make it harder to climb, but at least it did extend now to the top of the wall – just.

Cassie and Edward knew they had little time. The smoke was stinging their eyes and making them cough. But they had even less time than they realised, because the fire's progress through the attic floor was not gradual. Where smoke had poured between the boards, small flames had followed, and – suddenly, with a single gasping roar – almost the entire middle of the attic floor erupted at once into flame.

They had moved enough tiles to make a sizeable hole but the thin wooden laths still barred their way. Cassie set to work, wrenching at them, breaking them, tearing them apart, until there was a jagged space sufficient for them both to stand up and gasp thankfully at the cool air outside.

But they were not alone in seeking the fresh night air. The smoke was drawn that way too, engulfing them as it streamed around them and chimneyed out into the night.

At the edge of all this ruin the boy and the girl climbed out onto the roof, feeling alone and abandoned as the flames and smoke streamed past them. Once out, they found there was nothing to hold onto, no grip for their fingertips, nowhere for their heels to dig into – only a frantic scrabbling around to stop them from sliding helplessly down the steeply sloping roof. And there was nobody in the world to help them.

But at that moment there was a new sound – one that belonged to a different life, a safe life where only ordinary comfortable things happened. It was a sound that suggested dad getting ready to paint the kitchen ceiling, or mum wallpapering the landing. It was the homely clattering of a ladder being raised against a wall. Then the top of it appeared only a few yards away, reaching about a foot above the edge of the roof.

'Come on!' Edward shouted. But Cassie – in a sitting position, and trying desperately not to slide down – was almost paralysed with fear, and Edward had to do his rescuing firmly, taking one hand while her other felt instinctively around to find something to hold onto. There was nothing, no handhold. She had to force herself to move. He guided her patiently as she edged her behind slowly along the roof, and when they were at last level with the top of the ladder he persuaded her to turn over and move slowly, face down and feet first. He lay lengthwise on the impossibly sloping tiles so that he could hold her ankles and guide her bare feet, step by lowered step, onto the top rungs.

Once on the ladder Cassie took heart. She stepped cautiously down a few rungs, gripped tight, and waited while Edward – silhouetted black above her with the red crimson sky behind him – went through the same process and shifted from the rapidly disintegrating roof and onto the ladder.

Once there, however, he froze. Perhaps he couldn't cope with heights. Or perhaps he'd used up all his courage. What Cassie did then cost a lot in heroic effort. Gritting her teeth, she moved back up a few rungs and bent her body outwards so that she contained him, and he moved cautiously down from step to step, all the time in the apparent safety of her enclosing arms.

It was an illusion, of course. Edward was no safer that way. If he'd slipped and fallen, Cassie would not have been able to hold him. In fact, they would both have gone, plunging to the ground. But feeling is sometimes more important than reality.

It was slow. Cassie looked around her and took in everything with a visionary clarity brought on by danger. She saw there had been a change in the weather. The wind had dropped and the night had grown calmer. There were fewer clouds now, and a big full-faced moon gazed calmly down at her. Below them, she saw the raised faces of the other three, urging them down.

The fire had not yet finished its business. There was a calamitous thundering crash above them as the central part of the main roof disintegrated inwards in a great disastrous collapse. Tiles and woodwork crashed down on top of the fire below and a million savage sparks poured fiercely upwards, weaving and spiralling like swarms of red-hot insects flying heavenwards. There was a mighty *whooff* as air was sucked down. Big flapping banners of flame cracked and waved briefly in the sky. Some escaped and lived a brief life apart before they vanished.

Adam, wanting to speed them up, began to climb the ladder to meet them. But his extra weight made the base of the ladder sink into the soft earth. It lurched sideways and began to slip. He jumped off at once and the ladder stayed steady as the two rescuers climbed shakily down to the ground.

'We need to get away from the house!' Abigail said. Even with a brick wall between them and the fire, the heat was growing. The whole building might collapse at any moment.

So they backed away into the field. And as they did so they heard a gunshot. Then another. Then someone shouted, 'Don't move!'

Two cars arrived, and suddenly there were people everywhere. One of them was Sergeant Prater, handcuffed, firmly in the grip of Mr Tittipat's two men.

'You got him!' Abigail shouted.

'Yes,' one of them said bitterly. 'But too late.'

They didn't know what he meant.

'He's destroyed the evidence.' The man jerked his head to indicate the burning farmhouse.

'No, he hasn't,' Cassie said shakily. 'It's here. In this book.' She pulled the book from inside her shirt and handed it over.

'Well done, lad!' the man said.

That's the last time anyone is going to mistake me for a boy, Cassie thought. She was going to become herself again at the first opportunity.

From far away across the fields they heard the bells of a fire engine, and from all around them across the Fens the almost non-stop roar of hundreds of planes taking off.

Next morning, Mrs Barnes's big kitchen was crowded. There was to be no school that day for anyone, and there they all were, with Uncle Peter, Hilda Pritt, and young William. Abigail's mum – Mrs Barnes's best friend – was there as well, the two mothers leaning back against the dresser, side by side, with arms folded. Like twin sisters.

They're still not sure whether they're cross with us or proud of us, Molly thought.

Uncle Peter and Mr Tittipat had been talking in another room. Secret stuff, they supposed. Afterwards Uncle Peter came into the kitchen, hoping for a cup of tea. He still looked tired and drawn, but a bath, a night's sleep in a proper bed, and Mrs Barnes's full breakfast had restored his cheerfulness.

Molly glanced at Abigail. *He doesn't know what he's got coming to him*, she said without words. Abigail agreed.

All this time the wireless had been on, sleepily talking to itself in a low voice on the dresser. But then – everyone noticed it – there was a sudden change of tone, an interruption, and a more determined voice. *'This is the BBC Home Service. Here is a special bulletin, read by John Snagge.'*

John Snagge's voice was familiar to everyone in the country – all over the world in fact, wherever the BBC could be received. Molly noticed the tiniest pause before he went on, a small dramatic wait. You could tell he was going to say something important. Her mum reached across and turned up the volume.

'*D-Day has come! Early this morning the Allies began the assault on the north-west face of Hitler's European forces. The first official news came just after half-past nine when Supreme Headquarters of the Allied Expeditionary Force issued communiqué number one. This said: Under the command of General Eisenhower allied naval forces supported by strong air forces began landing allied armies this morning on the northern coast of France.*'

The news was electrifying. All over Britain, Molly thought with a shiver of excitement, people are saying to themselves *It's started! At last!*

Hilda, she noticed, bit her lower lip. *Has she*, Molly wondered, *a brother involved in the invasion? Or a boyfriend perhaps?*

She noticed her little brother, wide-eyed and grave, with his thumb in his mouth. And she saw Cassie look at Edward and Edward look at Cassie. They had got Uncle Peter out just in time.

But there were other things to think about. Later that day Cassie said to Uncle Peter, 'When are we going to move back into our own house?'

Uncle Peter looked uncomfortable. 'Cassie, there's something I have to tell you.'

'What?'

She knew something bad was coming because he hesitated. 'I have to go away for a while,' he said quietly.

'How long for?' Cassie asked, almost in a whisper. A week? Two weeks? She could bear that.

'Several months. Perhaps a year. I'm sorry, Cass, but . . .'

'Why?' she said quietly. I'm almost as tall as he is, she realised. My eyes are almost on a level with his. This change had crept up on her.

'I'm needed. I have to go with the allied army. As they advance into France and Germany, there will be agents and double agents everywhere, coming out of the woodwork. The authorities want me to check them. In some cases I'm the only person who will know how to question them.'

'You promised you'd never go away again!' In spite of herself, Cassie felt tears welling into her eyes. Something was being irreparably broken – and he didn't even know! Edward would have understood – but Uncle Peter was oblivious. 'You *promised*!' she said.

'Yes, I did. But, Cass, there's a War on. You know that. You've always understood that.' The old, old reason that everyone had used for five long years – *There's a War on*.

'You promised.' But her voice was low, defeated. She knew he would go whatever she said, however much fuss she made. He was a grown-up, he made his own decisions.

She turned her back on him.

Uncle Peter, a man ashamed, lowered himself slowly to sit on the arm of a chair. Cassie turned back to face him and realised as she looked down on him that for the first time in her life she was hiding from him what she felt and thought. She'd never done that before, not about anything that mattered.

'The world isn't perfect,' he said. 'I can't change that.'

'Then you shouldn't have promised.' She spoke quietly, severe and judgemental. *He* had taught her that! *He* had taught her never to lie, and never to make promises you couldn't keep.

'I know,' he said. But he didn't know, not really. He hadn't the faintest understanding of how her faith in the world had depended on him. 'In our family we keep our promises,' Cassie said, quoting his own words, reminding him of his betrayal.

He had nothing else to say. Was he distressed? Did he mind that he was being accused and judged? Cassie suspected he just wanted to escape, and have this embarrassing scene over and done with.

'What will happen to me while you're away?' Her voice was almost inaudible.

'I haven't quite worked that out. I did think . . .' he said cautiously, '. . . that you might become a boarder at St Dorothea's. Instead of a day girl.'

Cassie stared. 'No!' she said firmly. 'Absolutely not!'

The idea appalled her. 'Even if I said yes, what would happen in the holidays?'

'Surely,' said Uncle Peter, running his hands through his hair, 'among all those grief-stricken friends who turned up for my funeral there must be one – just one! – who would be prepared to take you.'

A few weeks ago, she might have stormed out of the room, shouting and slamming doors. But she left quietly and went in search of Edward. He would understand the loneliness of those words: *there must be someone who would be prepared to take you.*

The next day the five of them hurried to Mrs Burnside's shop and bought a copy of the *Daily Mirror*. They raced across town to Edward's house (he didn't want to go inside), then to the railway van. They settled inside on the bed to study the newspaper in cramped comfort.

Seven of the paper's eight pages were devoted to news of the invasion. The headlines were enough to make their spines tingle with excitement. DESTINY'S HOUR, said one. 300 SQ. MILES OF SOLDIERS, said another. And a third: GREAT ARMADA STRETCHED OVER HORIZON.

There was a message from General Eisenhower to every soldier, sailor and airman. *'The eyes of the world are upon you,'* he wrote. *'The hopes and prayers of liberty-loving people everywhere are with you.'* And there was a message from the king which they especially liked. *'At this historic moment surely not one of us is too busy, too young, or too old to play their part . . .'*

'Well, we've played our part,' Abigail said. And so had Uncle Peter's book of lies, for it was clear that the Germans had *not* concentrated their forces where the invading army had landed.

But there was a shadow on Edward's heart. Every day brought him closer to the time when he would have to go away. He wanted Cassie to know how unhappy he was, but at the same he did *not* want her to know. She had her own troubles.

On the cartoon page, the adventures of Popeye and Belinda continued as if nothing had happened. But Jane sat boldly naked on the edge of her bath, drying her back with a towel. Very badly drawn, Molly thought. The shading was clumsy and crude. Adam could have done it better.

Adam studied the Jane cartoon carefully. 'Your headmistress,' he said suddenly.

'Miss Sweetly? What about her?'

'Suppose she was right,' Adam said thoughtfully. 'About our Daisy.'

'*What* about Daisy?'

'That she's silly and childish.'

Abigail leapt to Daisy's defence. Molly just waited.

'Anyway,' Adam said, 'I've lost interest in her.'

Cassie joined in. 'But you can't just leave her stuck in Hitler's bunker.'

Adam thought. 'Well, I don't mind finishing this story,' he said. 'But then I'm going to stop.'

'From Hitler's bunker to Buckingham Palace in three strips!' Abigail said. 'Daisy can manage that.'

Molly, feeling depressed, agreed. But *why* had Adam lost interest in Daisy?

Adam was hopeless at explaining. But he showed them his latest sketchbook and they saw that it was filled with drawings of feet. Lots of feet! Molly recognised her own feet there, in several different versions. And Abigail's. And, further on, Cassie's too. But there were also the feet of a baby – upside-down because its legs were raised heavenward. And an old man's feet, twisted and knuckled and tough.

'Where did you find him?' Molly asked.

'He was sitting outside his house in Soham,' Adam said.

He's full of surprises, Molly thought. She saw at once that none of these feet had been drawn in the neat and precise way he'd done the Daisy drawings. They were sketchy, smudged, imperfect, inaccurate. But more *alive*.

There was one completed drawing – of a woman seated at a desk, looking up, intelligent, and attentive. The lines of her face and throat seemed to have sprung onto the page with their own energy and firmness. The rest was done in pastel colours, alive and vibrant, highlighted with white chalk. This one was alive too, like the feet.

'It's Miss Sweetly!' Abigail said in amazed delight. It *was* Miss Sweetly. No doubt at all.

'You can take it to school and give it to her if you like,' Adam said.

The cautious Molly was unsure, but Abigail said eagerly, 'Oh, *yes*! That will show her!'

(*But why*, Miss Sweetly wondered a few days later, *did he draw me with bare feet?*)

Cassie had a second conversation with Uncle Peter. The others were there too, a silent audience. Or witnesses perhaps.

'Who was Elizabeth Margaret Seymour?' Cassie said to him out of the blue.

Uncle Peter was taken aback. 'You know who she was! She was your mother.'

'But she wasn't your sister.'

He frowned, giving himself time to think.

'And you weren't my father's brother.' It was a statement, not a question. *He knows what's coming*, Molly thought.

'So you're not my uncle,' Cassie said quietly. 'Don't you think you'd better explain?'

'Explain what?' *His final attempt to get out of it*, Molly thought.

But there was no getting out of it. Cassie pushed home her point, sharply, so that there could be no fudging. 'I'm not your niece,' she said. 'And I'm not your adopted daughter. So what *am* I? *What am I doing here, with you?*'

There was tension in the room as they waited. Uncle

Peter took a deep breath. He saw that he was in the dock, and Cassie was his accuser.

'I loved your mother,' he said slowly. 'The three of us were best friends. We'd been friends ever since we'd been about six.'

Was he telling the truth? Or making it up?

'You young people today, you don't know anything about friendship. *Real* friendship, I mean. We did everything together, and we had no secrets from each other. But as we grew older both of us – your father and I – fell in love with your mother.'

A love story! This was meat and drink to Molly and Abigail. But not for Cassie. She felt as if she were being taken into another dark building full of danger.

'She chose your father, not me.'

His listeners waited. The room waited. The world outside had grown quiet and seemed to be waiting too.

'They were very happy. Eventually they had you – and you made their lives perfect. Then, as I've told you before, they were killed in a car crash when you were a few months old. Somewhere in Albania. I was in Greece when I got the news.'

He stopped. The path he'd been following had brought him to the edge of an abyss, and he was looking down into it. Molly saw the haunted look of sadness in his eyes. And she saw him take a deep breath before he went on. 'I went straight there. I found that the villagers had already buried your parents, and you were being looked after by a farmer's wife.'

Another pause. 'She was a very . . .' he hesitated, '. . . *fierce* woman. She had a baby of her own and she was breastfeeding both. Her twins, she said.'

Cassie wondered briefly if she had inherited some of the Greek woman's character by breastfeeding from her. She too was feeling fierce.

'She wanted to keep you, and so I told her I was your uncle. That's how it started. I gave her money and brought you back to this country, bought this house, and changed my job so that I could look after you.'

No, Cassie thought, *you didn't look after me*. That *was the old Uncle Peter*.

Molly was thinking about passports. And so was Cassie apparently, for she said to Uncle Peter, '*Can* you just walk out of a country with a baby that doesn't belong to you? Did I have a passport?'

'It wasn't a problem,' he said. 'The frontier in that country was a hit-and-miss affair. There were dozens of ways of getting out.'

How did he manage with baby feeding? Abigail wondered. *There was a story to be told here*, she thought. But Cassie was in too much hurry for details.

She frowned. 'What about getting into England? Surely a man can't just walk into this country carrying a baby girl without someone asking questions!'

Uncle Peter spoke quietly. 'You've forgotten what I did for a living. It was part of my job to get in and out of countries without being seen. I knew how to get that sort of thing done. Even with a baby.'

'And you told people I was your niece?'

He suddenly sat forward, facing her, speaking more firmly. 'It was easier that way. I was making it up as I went along. It was a difficult time. I'm sorry if you don't like it – *really* sorry – but it seemed the best thing to do.'

'And were you ever going to tell me the truth?'

'Of course I was!'

'*When?*'

'I was waiting for the right time,' he said. The two of them were connecting now. No more clipped and icy words.

They all flinched when Cassie suddenly shouted at him, '*Why* did you take me? You're not my father! You're not my uncle!'

He didn't shout back. 'I brought you here because I loved your mother. Then I came to love you.'

'You *stole* me!'

He rounded on her then, in anger. 'Stole you?' he said. '*Stole* you? Who from? *Who wanted you?*'

The farmer's wife perhaps, Molly thought.

Cassie stared at Uncle Peter. Then she left the room quietly, saying nothing. Edward got up and followed her. He wasn't sure she wanted him but he went anyway.

Cassie – wanting to be alone – went back later to the guest house to say thank you to Mrs Barnes. And there she came across Mr Tittipat. He immediately got up to make his escape.

She was as surprised as he was when she heard herself ask an abrupt question. 'Why couldn't you have told me Uncle Peter was alive?'

Mr Tittipat said in his horrible grating voice, 'We didn't know he was alive. But we did know that all manner of Nazi sympathisers were likely to come out of hiding to look for him.'

'So?'

'So we had to put the story to sleep. Quickly.'

'You could have saved me days and days of unhappiness,' she said.

'There is a War to be fought,' he said. 'It's rather important. Your feelings, on the other hand, are of no importance at all.'

She felt sore and distressed. 'All men seem to be liars!' she said.

He showed no surprise at this unexpected remark. 'Of course they are,' he said. 'Even your sainted Uncle Peter.'

'Women too, I suppose,' she said, making the most of her bitterness.

'Of course. But look on the bright side: you'll grow into it too, in time.'

And Edward? Will Edward, she thought, *turn into a liar?*

'But you're looking at it the wrong way,' he said.

'What do you mean?'

'You can't alter it. So you should turn it to your advantage.'

She frowned, waiting for more, disapproving.

'You have the moral high ground. Your uncle has lied to you and been found out – so *he's in your debt.*'

But how did he know about that? 'I was Peter's commander when he brought you home,' he said. 'I know the whole story. Now's your chance to get what you want. Tell him what you plan to do. Make your demands – and give him no choice.'

Cassie pondered.

'And don't waste time,' Mr Tittipat said. 'He feels very ashamed at the moment. But it won't last. It never does!'

He stood up to leave. 'When you see him, give him this, will you? It's of no further use to me.'

He handed her Uncle Peter's big book.

Dame Lily, Sir Tristram and Sergeant Prater had been taken away to prison. They were to be charged with treason, kidnap and conspiracy to murder.

When Sergeant Prater was questioned he clenched his teeth together like a barricade and refused to say a word. And Sir Tristram kept explaining to people how his country would be better off run by the Nazis. Dame Lily on the other hand talked freely to anyone who happened to be nearby – policemen, lawyers, warders, fellow prisoners. She rambled endlessly on, always telling the same story.

'It was my brother, you see. He admires Adolf Hitler. But he can't abide Churchill. *Loathes* him!

'– I danced with Hitler once, you know. In Berlin, before the War.

'– It was Tristram's idea that I should pretend to be in love with Peter Dinsdale. But I never found out anything useful. Peter was always too clever for me.

'– His book? Yes, I knew about his book. He showed it to me. Tristram said it was a slip-up on his part, and called him a silly ass.

'– Peter's a dear man, really. Deeply in love with me of course.

'– I phoned him, you know. That afternoon. Tried to warn him, but I was too late. Prater got there before he had time to get away.

'– They'll hang my brother, I suppose. He'd rather be shot by a firing squad, of course. Soldier's death.

'– Prater, too, I shouldn't wonder.

'– But we had some good times at first. At the start of the War. We ran a small spy-run. It was jolly risky! I managed it all, safe houses, German currency, everything! I found empty barns, outhouses, and that abandoned railway van. I did it all for Tristram, you know. I've always been under his thumb. Even when I was a child, I did everything he told me to do.

'– Information about troop movements, new airfields being built – it all went along my spy-run and ended up in Hitler's high command.

'– Only lasted about a year. Couldn't get people to cross the North Sea. Too big a risk, I suppose.

'– D'you remember a man called Creake? He

planned to blow up the whole of Great Deeping. No, that wasn't our idea. *He* thought of that. But it was me who arranged for the Jerries to drop carrier pigeons. He used them to send information back. Jolly clever! But it all came to nothing. He blew himself up instead of the town.

'– Prater was a good man, most of the time. The bonfire was his idea. He'd been building it for years.

'– I meant no harm, you know. And I didn't want anyone to get hurt. Do you suppose I'll get life imprisonment?

'– I'll never see St Dorothea's again. I *did* love those girls, you know. And I adored teaching them.

'– I wonder if they have drama groups in prison. Or poetry readings.

'– *Poor* Tristram! Will they let me say goodbye to him, d'you think? Before they . . . ?'

⇛

Edward wanted to attend his grandmother's funeral. It was unusual for children to do that but he was the old lady's only family. He was nervous but resolute.

'I'll come too,' Cassie said. 'And I promise not to run out in the middle of the service.'

'*I* might run out,' Edward said.

'I won't let you.'

Edward's face wore a look of such terrible bleakness when he took his position behind the coffin that Cassie stepped into place beside him, and walked with him.

It was against all custom, but she didn't care. And nobody stopped her.

But it wasn't as bad as Edward had feared. The Salvation Army band played three of his grandmother's favourite hymns. People who had known the old lady attended, and even more stood respectfully in the street.

The newspapers had not been allowed to report the story of the Ely spies. There was a War on, after all, and that sort of thing had to be kept quiet. Nevertheless, all the onlookers that afternoon knew that that nice Mr Dinsdale – who'd been buried a couple of weeks ago – was not dead after all; that his niece had run away from home and disguised herself as a boy ('*That* one there, the one with the short hair, walking beside the grandson!'); and that the kidnapped Peter Dinsdale had been found and rescued largely through the bravery and good sense of the children.

Mr Cheadle was there, of course, and with him the Woman from the Welfare. 'I have some news for you,' she said to Edward afterwards.

Cassie turned to move away, but she caught Edward's desperate look, and stayed.

The Woman from the Welfare knew this boy would not welcome what she had to tell him. But it had to be done, it was her job. 'There is a vacancy at the orphanage,' she said gently. 'The arrangements have been made.'

'When will I have to go?' Edward said.

'There's no point in putting it off.'

Edward stood with head bowed, like someone awaiting execution.

'The day after tomorrow,' she said. 'I'll take you up on the train.'

Not if I can help it, Cassie thought.

40
Cassie's Plan

'*What?*' Uncle Peter said to Cassie. 'What do you mean, *you don't want to live with me*?' Everyone listened, embarrassed but inquisitive.

It was not the best time for Cassie to make this announcement, for Uncle Peter had invited them all to a tea party as a thank you for rescuing him. 'I would have been a goner if it hadn't been for all of you,' he'd said.

'Isn't it obvious?' Cassie said. 'You *lied* to me. For thirteen years.'

'I didn't actually lie. I just never quite told you the full story.'

'Well, you're not who I thought you were. And now I'm not who I thought I was.'

'But nothing has changed,' he said. 'Unless you're determined to change it.' *He doesn't understand her,* Molly thought.

'It – was – a – lie. That book you wrote is all lies! Yes, I know it was part of the War. But lying comes naturally to you, you can't stop yourself. *And it was you who taught me always to tell the truth.* Now I feel as if everything that happened to me up to three weeks ago happened to someone else.'

She wasn't as in control as she seemed. Edward knew she was close to tears.

Then Uncle Peter shouted at her. '*CASSIE, I LOVE YOU!*' It was not said kindly, or affectionately. It came out like a battering ram. The others flinched. People never talked about *love* in their families – but if they had, they wouldn't have roared about it like that. Molly's little brother buried his face in her skirt because the Big Man was so *loud*.

Uncle Peter glared at Cassie. But she stood her ground, saying quietly, 'No, you don't! *That* was someone else! You're not him.' (Molly thought she'd never heard anything so sad in her life.)

He was shocked, they could tell. He spoke more quietly. 'I fell for you the moment I held you in my arms when you were a baby.'

'So you might have . . .'

'I loved you more than I've ever loved anyone.'

'Even Dame Lily?' Cassie said slyly.

'Dame Lily? I never loved her! That was just a way of keeping a close eye on her. I'd suspected her for years.'

Molly, the romantic, found that almost more shocking than everything else.

'Anyway, I have some demands.' Cassie was in control again.

'Demands? *What* demands?' (*Disbelief*, Molly thought.)

'You will have to get used to some changes. I want you to adopt me. Properly.'

'*Adopt* you? Whatever for?' (*Astonishment. Complete astonishment!*)

'If I'm going to live with you,' she said, 'I want to be your daughter.'

'What do you mean: *if* you're going to live with me? Of course you're going to live with me!' (*Now he's puzzled. A bit worried too.*)

'Not if you don't do what I want.'

'Where will you live then?' (*Scornful*, Molly thought, *but still worried.*)

'I'll run away.'

He folded his arms and looked at her as if she were an idiot. 'If you were about eight I might expect you to say something stupid like that. But you're *thirteen*. You know talk like that is just bluster.' (*He's wishing she were about eight!*)

'It's not. I have some money, I have my ration books. And I have someone to go with.'

Edward gaped. That was the first he knew about it.

'Who? How?'

'And don't think I'm making this up. Unlike you, *I don't lie*.'

'Oh, for heaven's sake!' (*Now he's getting angry,* Molly thought.)

'And that's not all. I want you to adopt Edward too. Or foster him.'

Edward looked from one to the other in confusion. He was feeling very little, *physically* little. He also felt a momentary longing for his old lost life, with his granny, and his railway van, and all his favourite things. Where no one shouted.

But Abigail's face lit up as she semaphored a message to Molly – *Brilliant! Absolutely brilliant!*

'*Edward!* Why should I want to adopt Edward?'

'Because he'll have to go to an orphanage if you don't. And because I want you to.' Then she added, sounding after all like an eight year old, 'I don't want him to go.'

Uncle Peter was sarcastic. 'The princess has escaped from the palace and has been mixing with the townspeople.'

Cassie became thirteen again – instantly. 'I am *not* a princess. And I *like* the townspeople! And I want Edward to live with us.'

'Aren't I enough for you?' (There was a touch of the pathetic in his words. Molly felt sorry for him – but only a little.)

'No, you're not,' Cassie said. 'I've been lonely for *years* – only I didn't realise it.'

'*Lonely?* But you had *me*?'

Cassie felt cruel. 'You're not enough. You probably were enough when I was five, but not any more.'

Uncle Peter looked from Cassie to Edward, and then from Edward back to Cassie. 'I was only away for a week or two . . . How could this . . . ?'

He didn't complete his question. *How could this totally unknown schoolboy have become so important to you?* Molly was sure that's what he'd intended to say.

'And there's another thing . . .'

'Oh! *Another* thing.'

'I was going to change schools. But I've decided to stay at St Dorothea's.' Then she added firmly, 'But not as a boarder.'

Cassie had thought a lot about St Dorothea's. The school was in trouble. When the news of Dame Lily's arrest spread, parents took their daughters away and sent them to other schools. But Cassie had a strong feeling of loyalty towards it. Dame Lily wasn't the only good teacher there, after all.

'This is absurd! I can't be made to adopt two kids – one of whom I don't even know!' (Molly recognised what he was doing. Her mother did it too – refusing something absolutely while working out in her head if it just might work.)

'Well, if you don't, I'll be off.' There was no apparent anger, no lasting wish to hurt him. Just a determined challenge.

There was a pause. Uncle Peter was still thinking it through. 'The authorities wouldn't let me adopt anyone.' (*I was right!* Molly thought triumphantly.)

'Why not? *Fostering* then. Fostering will do.'

'I'm not a suitable person.'

'No, you're not! But you can lie to them! You're good at lying!'

'But I told you – I have to go away again.'

'We can both stay at Mrs Barnes's guest house till you get back. She won't mind. Edward's there already. Though you'll have to pay our rent, of course.'

'You've worked it all out,' he said quietly.

'Yes, I have.'

'But . . .'

'It's just until you come back.'

'I've been warned about this.'

'Warned about what?'

'Thirteen-year-old girls having tantrums.' (*He's going to agree!* Molly thought.)

'Has it occurred to you,' Cassie said brightly, 'that a girl having a tantrum might still be in the right?'

Uncle Peter turned to Edward. 'Do you *want* to come and live with us? You don't have to be polite. Tell the truth. You can see what she's like!'

Despite his pretending and his daydreaming, Edward was a realist. It came to him in a flash of understanding that he should take this opportunity. And yet . . .

Cassie saw that something was troubling him. She took his arm and pushed him out into the hall. 'What's the matter?' she said. 'Tell me.'

Edward swallowed. There was no time for polite half-truths. He knew he must be honest with her. 'He scares me,' he said. 'He's so *loud*.'

Cassie frowned, searching for the best thing to say. 'I'm very angry with him at the moment,' she said. 'But he's a really kind man – and he *has* looked after me all these years.' Then she added, 'Three weeks ago I didn't know you existed.'

It was a strange thing to say and it made no sense.

But it did the trick. Edward made up his mind there and then, and they rejoined the others (much to their relief since none of them had known what to talk about without Cassie there).

Uncle Peter glared at Edward. 'Well? *Do* you want to live with us?' (*That might not be the best way of talking to Edward*, Molly thought.)

But Edward nodded. 'Yes.' Then, because he'd been brought up to be polite, he added 'Please.' It sounded a foolish word for such an important matter, as if he'd just been offered a biscuit.

'Of course he wants to!' Cassie said cheerfully. 'He's my hero!' They stood side by side.

'You do?' Uncle Peter said. 'Even now you've seen what a tyrant she is? She's ruthless!'

And that's another kind of lying, Molly thought. *Only he's teasing, so it doesn't count.*

Edward nodded vigorously.

'Good!' said Cassie. 'That's settled! Now let's all go outside and have our tea party.'

They've found their way through, Molly thought. She had a brief and vivid understanding – which she could never afterwards recapture – of loyalties and friendships holding people safe, even in tangles of falsehood.

'I almost forgot,' Cassie said. 'Mr Tittipat gave me this for you.'

It was Uncle Peter's big book. 'I shan't need that any more,' he said. 'Not now D-Day is over. It's no use to anyone now.'

As they turned towards the French windows, they became aware of a distant roar in the sky, approaching low. Alarmingly low. They rushed outside and stared up.

A Lancaster bomber, barely above the rooftops, grey and battered, was piling its colossal weight skywards. Everywhere shook. It was so low that they could clearly see helmeted heads in the cockpit. Two, was it? Or three? And one of the figures waved. The plane's huge wide-winged shadow flickered over the garden, briefly engulfing the watchers on the ground. Once past them, the Lancaster rapidly gained height. And in a few moments the sound of its four big engines faded into the silence of the sky.

And that, Molly thought, was Hilda saying goodbye. It meant: *Well done, you lot! Glad to have been a part of what you did. But it's wonderful to be flying again. Bye! Toodle pip!*

Well, something like that.

Uncle Peter said aside to Cassie, 'It won't be the same, you know.'

'I should hope not!' she retorted.

'And you, young man? Are you quite sure?'

'Abso-bloomin-lutely!' Edward said.

Inside, Uncle Peter's big book was still on the table where Cassie had left it, lying.

In the months leading up to the D-Day landings three armies were being assembled in Britain. Two were fictitious.

As hundreds of thousands of men were secretly gathering along the south and south-west coast and preparing to invade Normandy, extraordinary efforts were made to convince the Germans that there were two other armies – one in Scotland preparing to invade Norway, and the other in East Anglia and Kent, preparing to invade France in the Pas-de-Calais region at the narrowest point of the English Channel. The aim of this massive deception was to attack where Hitler least expected it, and to ensure that his great concentrations of enemy forces were in the wrong places. So successful was this deception that, even after the invasion, Hitler continued to believe that the Normandy landings were a diversion and that the main attack would soon occur near Calais.

Dozens of ingenious ideas supported this strategic trickery, but the most important was the leaking of what was called *wireless traffic* – thousands of radio messages between the military personnel responsible for assembling these phantom armies. While this was going on the British authorities did everything in their power to ensure that everyone in the country understood the importance of secrecy. People became almost obsessed with the idea that *careless talk cost lives* and that even a casual remark about a passing army convoy might somehow find its way to German high command and be useful there.

As far as I am aware, there was no single person responsible for the radio transmissions. Uncle Peter – like all the characters in this story – is entirely fictional. St Dorothea's School in Ely is also fictional. However, the other school, attended by Molly and Abigail, did exist (and still does today under a different name and on a different campus), but it never had a headmistress called Miss Sweetly. Even before the national eleven-plus examination came into operation after the War, there were schemes throughout the country to enable children to win scholarships to attend their local grammar or high school. This is how Molly and Abigail came to be pupils at the Ely High School.

Hilda's put-down to her male superior ('I *fly* the bally thing. I don't have to *carry* it!') is based on fact. According to Giles Whittell's excellent book *Spitfire Women of World War II*, the ATA pilot Rosemary Rees said something similar to a wing commander when he expressed surprise that a woman of five foot three and seven stone weight could fly a 30-tonne Avro York.

For more adventures featuring Molly,
Abigail and Adam . . .